I'll Sing You One-O

by Nan Gregory

Clarion Books
New York

The author would like to thank the Canada Council for the Arts
for its support during the writing of this novel.

Clarion Books
a Houghton Mifflin Company imprint
215 Park Avenue South, New York, NY 10003
Copyright © 2006 by Nan Gregory

The picture book referred to on pages 148 and 163 is *Mysterious Thelonious*
by Chris Raschka (New York: Orchard Books, 1997).

The text was set in 12-point ITC Legacy Serif Book.

For information about permission to reproduce selections from
this book, write to Permissions, Houghton Mifflin Company,
215 Park Avenue South, New York, NY 10003.

www.houghtonmifflinbooks.com

Printed in the U.S.A.

Library of Congress Cataloging-in-Publication Data

Gregory, Nan.
I'll sing you one-o / by Nan Gregory.
p. cm.
Summary: Reunited with her long-lost twin brother, twelve-year-old
Gemma constantly tests the boundaries of acceptable behavior while
relying on angels to help her connect with her new family.
ISBN-13: 978-0-618-60708-2
ISBN-10: 0-618-60708-0
[1. Foster home care—Fiction. 2. Brothers and sisters—Fiction.
3. Twins—Fiction. 4. Conduct of life—Fiction.]   I. Title. II. Title:
I will sing you one-o.
PZ7.G86235Il 2006
[Fic]—dc22
2005032709

MP 10 9 8 7 6 5 4 3 2 1

For Sheila Egoff, whose keen vision inspired me through the first years of Gemma's quest, and for Dinah Stevenson, who sparked me to journey's end. If there be angels, look down, Sheila, and see me now.

one

"I'll sing you one-o,
Green grow the rushes-o,
Oh, what is your one-o?
I'll sing you two-o,
Green grow the rushes-o,
Oh, what is your two-o?
I'll sing you three-o . . ."

I'm out behind the hen house hanging on as hard as I can to Pippi Longstocking, who is squawking her head off and struggling to get free of my lap. My eyes are squeezed shut, and I'm singing the question song at the top of my lungs. I have it in my mind that if I sing it to a hundred without stopping and without opening my eyes, the faces on the other side of the chicken-wire fence will disappear, and I'll be safe to stay here on the farm forever. This is my first try at sorcery, but right now magic seems my only chance.

I sing to ten and open my eyes a squint. They're all still there, staring in at me. Beloved Mr. A. and Mrs. A. and Jess and Arlie and Darren and Meg. My poppy-faced, alleged Uncle Dave; my freckle-blotched, so-called Aunt Moira—the Burdettes.

"Moe-EYE-rah." Moira said it very clearly and precisely when we were introduced just minutes ago in the front yard. "Moe-EYE-rah." Making sure I'd get it right next time.

She waited for me to say it, so I did. "Moe-EYE-rah."

"Good," she said. "Now run it together: Moira." Then she smiled with her thin lips drawn back and her teeny, perfect teeth shut tight. It was the click of them coming together that sent me fleeing through the house and into the chicken yard.

The third Burdette, my scrawny, supposed-to-be twin brother, Garnet—and what kind of a name is that?—clings half hidden behind her, as if the sight of a girl scrunched in the corner of a chicken coop invoking a spell to blast him to atoms is a horror beyond his wildest imaginings.

I clamp my eyes closed again and sing harder. Pippi squalls. The rest of the chickens cluck up a protest. The rooster crows manfully. They are unused to me in my sorcerer mode. They don't care for my noise. We are all singing for our lives.

> "I'll sing you twenty-o,
>   Green grow the rushes-o . . ."

I hear the gate squeak inward. Pippi is batting me frantically with her wings and pecking at my face with her poor, bent beak. Her legs, which are astonishingly strong, gallop against my body. I let her go out of pity for her panic, and wad myself up into a ball.

"I'll sing you twenty-five-o . . ."

Someone's arms lock around me and hug me hard. It's Mr. A. I can tell from the smell, field and fresh sweat, and the brush of his mustache on my cheek. I keep myself curled against his chest and slow down my singing to the rhythm of his heart beating under my ear. If he and I both wish as hard as we can, surely we can magic things back to the way they were before.

He lets me get through thirty. Then he gives me a little shake and tells my ear "Enough" in a quiet, anything-more-means-war-with-me voice. I'm not against him. It's for love of him, and Mrs. A., and my foster sibs, Jess and Arlie and Darren and little Meg—for the whole farm—that I'm doing this. And now he's saying no.

He holds my hand back to the house. We count under our breaths together, "One thousand one, one thousand two, . . ." He taught me thousands when I first came to the farm, back when I was four. I arrived not talking at all, just singing the question song over and over as high as I could count and throwing tantrums all over the place. Mr. A. saw right away how I like numbers and showed me that counting thousands was better than bursting into fury at the bristle of every little hair.

Numbers are still good for calming me down. They're steady and come in a reliable order, and you can depend on them always staying the same. Thinking this doubles me over because of how everything else is falling apart, and I lose count, and Mr. A. lifts me to my feet and waits until I'm ready to walk.

In the kitchen, Mrs. A. disinfects the chicken scratches on my bare legs, spruces the straw and feathers off my T-shirt, and sends me to change into a clean pair of shorts. Arlie holds Meg in her arms and shushes her whimpers. Darren and Jess watch from the doorway. Jess's fingernail goes *skrrrr, skrrrr* up and down the screen door. No one says, "Quit making that creepy noise" or "Cut that out," the way they usually do. No one says anything, because there's nothing left that we haven't said a million times. *Goodbye, goodbye, sorry, sorry, miss you, miss you.*

Once I'm all neatened up again, Mrs. A. brushes a brisk kiss on my forehead. I go to flood into her arms, but she holds me away. Mr. A. picks up my suitcases and leads us across the yard to the shiny new van where my fake family waits for me in shocked and icy stillness.

I climb in. The door rolls shut. The electric window hums up, and I see my beloved true family dimmed away by the faint green of the glass. I wave and wave. The van bounces down the long rutted driveway and turns past the FOR SALE sign we kids cursed and kicked at every day all summer long. I look back. The farmhouse is tiny at the top of the rise. I think I can see Jess, still waving.

The van picks up speed. Farmlands rush past the window, blur to a washrag, and wipe away my life as ever I've known it.

two

The Burdettes' house sits huge and proud, high above the street. "We've just had it painted," Moira tells me, and points out how the daisies that flank the long steps perfectly match the yellow of the front door. It's all polish and smoothness, not one crack or chip to take the edge off its smug, face-lifted face. The house on the farm is friendly and worn, and the flowers there choose their own bright colors.

Inside the yellow door there's an entrance hall for coats and shoes. "The farm has a mudroom, too," I say. "Ours is around back."

Moira tells me it's a foyer ("FOY-ay"), not a mud-room, and sure enough, there's not a speck of dust, let alone a blob of mud, anywhere to be seen. I flop my sneakers into the corner and get shown right away how to line them up neatly on a little tray beside everyone else's.

"We thought you'd like a quick tour of the house

before we take you to your room," Dave says, and we all fall into line behind Moira. First doorway on the left is Dave's study, stuffed with books, and across the hall is the living room and the piano, which nobody touches but Garnet. Past that, through an archway, is the dining room. The air is sharp with a blaring lemony smell. Everything glows and shines. The polish on the dining room table looks as deep as a lake of molasses. I have to test if I can dip my finger in. Moira scrubs away my fingerprint with the cuff of her sleeve.

"You should have seen what a mess it was before the renovations," she says.

"Your Aunt Moira has very high standards," Dave says, "but I think she's finally satisfied." He puts an indulgent arm around her shoulders. "It's been a long haul." She cuddles in, tiny beside his big bulk. Mrs. A. is as tall as Mr. A. and stands on her own.

The back of the house is one big glassy room, with a kitchen at one end and a computer station and the biggest TV I've ever seen at the other. A canary chirps forlornly from a cage hanging by the side window. I go over for a little hello.

"That's Petey," Dave tells me.

"He's cheery, isn't he?" Moira says. How can she think he's cheery? He's in a cage! She sees the question in my face and answers it. "He's yellow. I always find yellow such a cheery color."

"Your aunt loves yellow," Dave says.

I'm rescued from erupting that a bird is a person,

not an ornament, by a *rap-tap-tap* on the glass doors. Moira hurries over to unlock them, and the bright, weathered face of an old woman peeks through.

"I won't come in," she says. "I thought you might like some lovely fresh green beans." She hands over a basket and peers around curiously.

"Do come meet Gemma," Moira says.

"Well, just for a moment." She shakes off pink plastic gardening shoes and hops in barefoot.

"This is Gemma," Dave says, and tries to put his hands on my shoulders. I duck out from under, and he lets me go with an embarrassed laugh. "Gemma, this is Dulcie Waldron. She's our next-door neighbor and dear friend."

I don't say anything, and Dulcie says, "So this is Garnet's long-lost sister. I do hope you'll be happy here, my dear."

I feel like shouting at her that I'm no sister of his, and I was happy where I was, and I'm going back there just as soon as ever I can—but it's not her fault, she didn't bring me here, so I clench my teeth and shriek silent thousands in my head.

She backs up a step and turns her smile on Moira. "I noticed you were a little late coming home, so I took the liberty of whipping up some dinner for you."

There's a strangled sound from behind me, and I look back to see Dave and Garnet exchanging panicked glances. Moira says right away how kind it was of her, and Dulcie beams and says she'll bring it over in a little while. I can feel Dave and Garnet bursting to say something, but Moira hustles us out of the kitchen, hissing fiercely, "Not one word! From anyone! I've just about had it today, and Dulcie was very kind . . ."

Up the stairs we go, to a long sleek-floored hall on the second floor. My first thought is, What a great place for sock hockey! Then it collapses in on me that Jess and the others will never see it, and I'm stuck here alone among strangers. Tears prickle the back of my nose, and that makes me sneeze.

"You're not getting a cold, are you?" Moira asks.

"No." So what if I were?

She ushers me around the master bedroom. They have two closets, big as whole rooms, stuffed with clothes, and a private bathroom with two sinks and two toilets—disgusting!—and a tub sunk into the floor. Next door is Moira's study, which is mostly empty. "A room of one's own," she says, and does a little pirouette right there in the middle of it. Then she blushes and hustles us across to Garnet's room. Here's something amazing: Almost one whole wall is fish, gliding and darting and flipping through the dark water of a tank that reaches nearly to the ceiling.

"We had to reinforce the floors for that sucker," Dave tells me proudly.

I start over for a closer look, and Garnet says, "She can't just come in here, can she? Poking around? Tell her she can't."

It's the first time I've heard him speak. His voice is needle-thin, a perfect match for his spindly body. I've read that boy and girl twins aren't identical, so there's no real reason why he and I should look alike, but even so, I can't compute how I could be related to someone so flimsy. He must be twelve, because that's how old I am, but he's barely as tall as my shoulder. His clothes aren't exactly too big, but he tucks himself away small inside them, as though he's keeping his real self secret. He has a pointed little chin and a wide mouth, and his ears stick out. His hair is a dirty blond and his eyes are huge and vividly green. An insect face.

"Garnet's right," Moira says. "We respect each other's privacy in this house. We don't go into each other's rooms unless we're invited."

At the farm we're always in each other's rooms. One time Mr. A. took our doors right off their hinges because we wouldn't stop slamming them, and we had no doors at all for over a month. We don't mind about privacy at the farm.

Next door is the bathroom Garnet and I are meant to share. The tub is a regular size, and I'm relieved to see there's only one toilet.

Moira points out a rack with a pile of neatly folded pink towels on it. "These are yours. The blue ones are Garnet's." She smoothes the wrinkles out of a blue towel and says in a warning voice that includes him, too, "Do make sure to stretch them out well to dry. Once they get mildewed, they're ruined. You can wash them until you're blue in the face, but as soon as they get wet, they'll start reeking all over again."

At the end of the hall is a narrow door that opens onto a set of steep stairs. It stops being shiny here.

Dave holds one of my suitcases in front and one behind as he climbs. "What have you got in here?" he asks. "Bricks?" Sweat is popping out on his forehead.

"Books, mostly."

"You're a reader, then."

I give him a "Hmm" that he can take either way. It's not any of his business what a great reader I am.

"That's my good girl."

I'm not his any kind of girl.

three

We safari through the attic, past boxes and trunks and shelves of books and piles of I don't know what and what I suppose must be clothes racks draped in sheets. At the far end there's a zigzag wall of screens with a curtained entrance. We all squeeze through.

"This is your room," Moira says.

I go right to its little window and kneel down to look out. Through the leafy branches of a huge maple tree I can see the houses opposite, and beyond them, in the distance, mountains and sky. I imagine myself running down the street, running, running, getting smaller and smaller until I'm nothing at all.

"What do you think?" Moira calls my attention back and points out the bed, tucked in where the ceiling slants down, the little table beside it decked with a frilly lamp, the desk, the rug, the shelves, the dresser, the beanbag chair. "It's a pink motif," she tells me. It certainly is. Everything in the place is either pink or white, flowered, striped, dotted, plain. She opens a boxy wardrobe, and I see wild-haired me reflected in the mirror on the door, the only unhappy thing in a bright, peppermint world. "What do you think?" she asks again.

At the farm I almost always share a room with someone. All I can think is how lonely it will be, way up here at the top of the house.

Dave relieves us of my silence. "I've got something you might like," he says, and disappears through the curtain. Moira and I stare at each other uncomfortably. Garnet circles the room poking at stuff with Hansel-thin fingers. There's a rustling and a clunking from beyond the screens, and the sound of heavy scraping. Then Dave says, "Where is that darn thing?" and something falls over.

"I do apologize about not having proper walls," Moira says. "Your coming was such a rush. We wanted to get you settled in before the beginning of the school year, so we simply had to make do with screens. I've hung scarves over them, but we can pretty them up with posters if you like."

"I always wanted my room up here," Garnet says.

"Don't be silly. You have a perfectly beautiful room!"

I can see Garnet taking breath for another round, but Dave breezes triumphantly in. His face is glowing. "Found it!"

He holds out a small book with a faded cover. I recognize it right away—*Charlotte's Web*. It just happens to be my favorite story in all the world, even though some people might say it's too babyish for me at my age. I've read it at least a dozen times—three of them out loud to Pippi Longstocking. I always thought I was like Fern, and Pippi was my Wilbur, because I rescued her from the pet store when she was just a chick. She had a bad infection in her beak, and they were going to put her down. Mrs. A., who was like Mrs. Arable in the story, said she didn't think Pippi would pull through, but I nursed her and nursed her, and look what a fine figure of a hen she is now!

Dave waggles the book invitingly. I have my own copy of *Charlotte's Web*. It's in my suitcase with my other books. Mine's just a paperback, but I don't care. I don't need his. I knot my hands behind my back and glare my uninterest from underneath my bangs.

"It used to belong to your mom," he says. "Look here. She's written her name in it."

My hands reach out.

The writing is clumsy. "Ruby Rain Burdette, age 8. This is my best book."

Ruby Rain. I make the words silently with my tongue. I never heard such a beautiful name. Soft feelings start rising up, and the chasm that comes when I let myself wonder about my mom. I start singing the question song in my head to clamp the feelings back, but I can't stop myself from asking, "How come you have this book?"

"It was one of the things she left behind. It's a long story."

He lowers himself onto the bed. The springs groan a protest and the mattress sags into a V around his blobby body. He grins sheepishly, heaves himself up, and moves to the chair by the desk. With a brisk sweep of her hand, Moira banishes the wrinkles he left on the quilt. He leans forward, hands clasped together. "Let me tell you about Ruby."

"I'll go down and see what I can do to rescue dinner," Moira says, and whisks herself away.

I half feel like escaping, too, but I'm needy with longings to hear what Dave has to tell.

four

Dave stares into the cup of his hands as though it holds a picture of what he's going to say. The hair on the top of his head is as thin and dull as a worn-out teddy bear's. It must be awful to have such poor hair—not the least like Mr. A.'s wild curls, which he mostly pulls back into a long ponytail. After some little while of thinking, Dave looks up. His eyes are small and droop at the edges, like sad old doggie eyes. There was a dog on the farm once with eyes like that. He could get anything from you just by staring at you.

I steel myself against feeling sorry for Dave. He's not the one around here deserving sympathy.

He clears his throat, and I come alert. Now he's going to tell me about my mom. *I'll sing you one-o.* The good thing about the question song is that it has no answers. There's no danger of finding out what you don't want to know. Now, answers about my mom are coming. I keep the song going so I can hear them from far away.

Dave sighs and begins. "My parents tried for years to have a baby of their own. Finally, they gave up and decided to adopt. Of course, they wanted an infant, but babies are hard to come by, so they agreed to take an older child. Ruby was five when they got her. Almost immediately my mom got pregnant with me. It happens like that sometimes."

"What was she like?" Even my own voice sounds small and thin through the distance of the question song.

"She used to read to me. And sing. She loved to sing, I remember."

"Was she pretty?"

"Oh, yes, very. I used to think I had the most beautiful sister in the world. She had long dark silky hair and big green eyes. Garnet has them, too. What color are yours?" He reaches out to push back my bangs.

I flinch away. I don't let people touch my hair. "What else?"

"She was always wild, wasn't she, Dad?" Garnet is hovering in the doorway. I forgot he was here. I shoot him a mind-your-own-business glare, but he doesn't budge. "Wasn't she?"

Dave sighs. "When she got to be a teenager, she began to run away. My mom and dad would hunt for her, bring her home. She'd stay for a little, and then she'd be gone again. We never knew why. For some reason no one could figure out, she simply became a stranger. When she was seventeen, she disappeared for good. We didn't know if she was dead or alive.

"I was only seven when it started, so I didn't really understand what was going on. All I knew was that I missed her terribly. From then on, and for all the time I was growing up, her not being there was the biggest presence in the house. Even when my parents gave up looking, it was like a shadow at the center of our home, missing Ruby."

I nod. It's a shadow in the center of me, too.

"And you didn't see her again until . . ." Garnet prompts. Now he's sitting at Dave's feet. "Tell her about that, Dad."

Dave shifts his shoulders around as if he's uneasy with what's coming next. "I grew up, met Moira at law school. We got married and bought this house. Late one night the doorbell rang, and there was Ruby. Fifteen years of no word, no nothing, and there she was, on my doorstep at one in the morning with a pair of just-about-newborn twins in her arms. A boy and a girl. You, Garnet, and you, Gemma." Dave smiles kindly at each of us. "Her two jewels, she called you."

So that's where Garnet's name came from. "Same as her," I say. "She was a jewel, too. Ruby." Except a garnet's really only just a stone.

"That's right," Dave says. "Three jewels."

I glance over at Garnet. Our eyes meet like marbles clinking.

"Tell her the rest," Garnet says.

"She was in rough shape. We took her in, of course, but it rapidly became clear that she couldn't stay. Moira and I had recently lost a baby of our own. We'd been told we'd never be able to have another, and we weren't in such good shape ourselves. Ruby asked us if we'd keep her babies for her. There was no way we could've handled both of you, but Garnet wasn't well, and we agreed to take him. She took you away, Gemma, and that was the last we saw of you or of her. We hunted night and day, but you might have fallen off the face of the earth for all we could find out—just like when Ruby was seventeen." He reaches out and tousles Garnet's hair. "Garnet's been with us ever since, and he's been nothing but a blessing. We have a son, as good as if he'd been born to us. We're enormously grateful for that." Garnet snuggles his head up like a patted puppy.

I hold my mom's book tight to my middle and rock against the pressure of it. Longings are seeping in. I stamp my foot against them. Dave looks up, startled, and continues with the story.

"Fast-forward twelve years. One day last month, Social Services called us out of the blue and told us they had you. They said you'd been found at the age of four abandoned in a room in the Downtown East Side, and that you'd been fostered out at Andersen Farm ever since. Eight years it took them to bother to track us down! They said the farm was being closed as a foster facility, and asked us if we'd be willing to take you. Of course we said yes." He looks as though he wants to tousle me, too. I step back. "I know this has been hard on you," he says, "but we're confident that it won't be long before you settle in and feel at home here."

I stare at him through the hedge of my bangs. "Ruby was adopted, right? She wasn't your real sister. So you're not really my uncle, right? We're not really related."

He shakes his head and splays his hands like it's so obvious, why can't she see it? "Your mother was the only sister I ever had. I loved her. Family is more than blood connections, Gemma."

Doesn't he think I know that? Doesn't he get it that the farm people are my family, not this houseful of kidnappers? "And besides, my mom would never abandon me."

"No, of course not." He stands up. "We'll leave you here to unpack and get a feel for your room. When you're done, come on down. Dinner should be pretty soon."

I hear their footsteps fading out as they go down the attic stairs.

What I feel like doing right this minute is taking off for the farm. I could do it, too. I know how to get there. You just ask a bus driver. But it's no good just blindly running home. Jess told me all about what happens to runaways. First they take you back to where you ran from and fake this kind and understanding act to get you to adjust. Then if you don't adjust and they can't cure you of running, they put you in Lockup, which is a kind of kids' prison, and if you manage to escape from that and they catch you, they chain you to your bed until you're eighteen and the law makes them let you go. By then you're an animal with scars where they handcuffed you and welts where they beat you, and there's nothing left for you but a life of drugs and crime. So I have to be canny and bide my time until I figure out a plan. I would die if they put me in chains.

I sit on the bed and open up *Charlotte's Web* again. There's my mom's signature. Ruby Rain. I trace the letters with my fingers. My mom's hand held the pen that made those marks. It's the closest I've been to her since before I can remember. The letters push bumps through to the back of the page. I did that, too, when I was eight, pressed too heavily trying hard to be neat. Where's my mom now?

Longings rise up. *I'll sing you one-o* . . . I close the book and slip it under my mattress. Maybe Garnet will let me look at his fish.

He doesn't seem too happy to see me, even though I remember to knock before I let myself in. He's curled on his bed, drawing something on a pad of paper. When I go over, he closes it away hurriedly and sits on it. What do I care? I wander over and kneel down by the fish tank.

The longer I look into the dark water, the more different kinds appear, striped and spotted and iridescent plain, kissing the empty water, nibbling around in the gravel, veiling themselves among the wavy leaves. There's a speckled fellow with big independent eyes who flutters his fins in a trembling blur, and a golden pair with tails like drifting scarves. But the enchantment is how they flick and glide, how they suspend themselves, not up, not down, weightless and serene in the water. It seems so effortless. Then I discover that if I twist my head up I can see the bottom of the top of the water where the whole dreamy fish dance is reflected upside down.

I get all drifty thinking how odd it is to be looking at the bottom of the top of something. The only sound in the room is the soft burble and hum of the tank. It feels sweet and sad and friendly, and I turn to Garnet and ask, "Do you ever miss our mom?"

He sits up all stiff and proper, pooches out his bottom lip, and says, "Moira's my mom."

I count thousands into the hall, turn my socks so the heel holes are on top, and slide around on the shiny floor until we get called to dinner.

five

A large casserole dish sits in the middle of the kitchen table. Moira thumps a big bowl of green beans in front of Dave and says, "I've asked Dulcie to join us for dinner." Then she turns to me. "Why don't you sit here, on this side? And Garnet, bring a chair for Dulcie, will you please?"

Dulcie waits for Garnet to wheel the computer chair over to the table, simpers a girlish thanks, and sits down beside Garnet. "Shall I serve?" she asks.

"Please do," Dave says. We pass our plates up.

Dulcie takes the top off the casserole dish. "I hope you like macaroni and cheese," she says. I do. It's one of my favorites. She plops a big spoonful on a plate and gives it to Dave to add beans.

"How does this look for you, Gemma?" he asks, and places it in front of me.

It's paler than the kind I get at home. A kind of water is oozing out around the edges. "What brand is this?" I ask, just to be polite.

I can feel a snicker running around the table. My face goes hot.

"Goodness!" Dulcie says. "It's not from a package!"

"Whole-wheat?" Dave asks, pushing a piece of macaroni around with his fork.

"I hope you don't mind," Dulcie says.

"It's delicious," Moira says meaningfully.

"Gives it a certain texture," Dave says. "Hearty."

"At my age, a person can't afford empty calories," Dulcie says, and turns to me. "How old would you say I am?"

A hundred? Her face is all covered with lines. A thousand?

"You'll never guess—eighty-five! I keep active—that's how to stay young."

"You're an inspiration," Dave says. "You really are."

"I thought we were having chicken wings," Garnet whines.

"We got home a little too late to make chicken wings," Moira says, with a warning flick of her eyes toward me. I know what that flick means. It means they would have been home on time if a certain someone—namely, me—hadn't screwed things up by having a tantrum in the chicken yard. But it's not my fault. If they hadn't come out there in the first place, they could have stayed home and made chicken wings all afternoon.

After that no one says much for the rest of the meal, except Dulcie, who explains in great detail about some new invention she's found for growing tomatoes upside down.

Moira clears the dinner plates. "Good girl," she says to me. "You finished it all up." Dulcie beams at me. I beam back. I'm a total wizard at getting rid of food. At the farm we have to eat everything on our plates, and if we don't get it all down at one meal, we're faced with eating it at the next. All us farm kids are experts at sneaking food into our napkins and dumping it at school the next day. The napkins are paper on the farm. This cloth one holds a lot more.

"How about some empty calories?" Dave says. "Anyone for brownies?" He's up and rummaging around in the cupboards. "Do you like chocolate, Gemma? Garnet and I make the chocolatiest brownies west of the Rockies. Come over here, son, and give me a hand."

When the brownies are out of the oven, Dave settles us down to watch a video of *The Wizard of Oz*. "It's my favorite movie," he tells me. "We only bring it out for special occasions." He puts his arm around Moira, and gives me a little smile over her head. Dulcie arranges a nest of cushions in a big chair and curls up like a kitten. Garnet says he doesn't want to watch *The Wizard of Oz* for the millionth time, so he's allowed to play games on his cell phone as long as he turns off the volume. I've seen it two million times myself, but I don't mind watching it again because Dorothy gets back home in the end, and that's what I want more than anything, too.

At the first taste of the brownies, I realize how hungry I am. I eat and eat, consoled by their sweetness. Dave praises my capacity. "When you're young, you can get away with it." He smiles ruefully and pats his paunch. Mr. A. is very thin. He gets away with eating whatever he wants.

Then it's bedtime. Moira follows me up to my room. "You haven't unpacked," she says, and sweeps my clothes out of the suitcases and folds them away, *tsk*ing over every little tear and hole. "What do you sleep in?" she wants to know.

"That big T-shirt."

She sighs and hands it to me. She seems to be waiting for me to get undressed, which I'm not doing in front of her, not for anything. I face her down until she gets the idea and tells me to put my dirty clothes in the laundry hamper and she'll collect them in the morning. Nothing I've got on is dirty enough to deserve washing, but I don't bother to say so.

"Get a good night's sleep," she says. "Tomorrow we'll go shopping for school. We'll buy you some nice new clothes." She's staring at my socks. I follow her gaze and see the heel holes are still on top from when I was sliding in the hall.

I don't like this place. I want to go back to where I feel good enough.

I'm locked in a fish tank in front of the farmhouse. Pippi Longstocking is outside, beating her wings on the glass and shrieking, "Ruby! Ruby! He's got Ruby!" I open my mouth to scream, and water rushes in. Then I'm outside, trying to run, but there are fish all over the ground, and I slither and skid and fall. I can hear my mom calling for help, and wicked-witch music. Dun-ta run-ta run-run. Dun-ta run-ta run-run. Then I'm in the barn, and Red Boy towers over me. He's spitting balls of fire and brandishing my mom in his claws. I can't see her face, just her long hair waving back and forth. "Help," she cries. "Help me, Gemma!" I hack at Red Boy's scaly foot with the FOR SALE sign until it splinters into toothpicks. He laughs wickedly and reaches down to pluck me up. "You!" he shouts. "I'll have you, too!"

I wake screaming in a tangle of wet sheets, Dave and Moira's worried faces bobbing above me. They don't know how to hold me like Mr. A. does, so I have to flail and pant and scramble my legs around until I calm my own self down. Of course, I don't tell them what the trouble was. I never say Red Boy's name out loud. That would give him too much power. So I get put in the bath while Moira changes my sheets, which is an awful embarrassment being as how I'm way past the age for that kind of thing. Then they put me back to bed and promise that nightmares don't come twice in one night. They don't know Red Boy.

As soon as I roll over, I hear the crickle-crackle of plastic, and I know they've put some baby sheet underneath me in case I wet the bed again. I don't need that! I jump up and pull everything off the bed—pillows, blankets, sheets, shameful plastic pee protector—and when I'm done, I'm limp and sad and far too downhearted to make the bed again. I wrap myself in my blankets and kneel at the little window. Over the trees, over the rooftops, dark on dark, far off where the shadow of the mountaintops blocks out the stars, I see a weird thing— a bright question mark shining in the night. I don't know if it's real or if it's magic. I can't imagine what question the mountains might be asking themselves. Mine is this: How come, when I have to leave everything I love behind, the thing that follows me is what I fear the most?

Next thing I know, I wake with my head on the windowsill and it's morning.

six

School is still a week away. Moira and Dave are working, so Garnet and I get sent to day camp down the street. Most of the kids are way younger, and it's like kindergarten jail after the freedom of the farm—cooperative games in the weeny park by the community center, "Careful, don't throw those balls too hard now," paddling in the wading pool, "Don't splash! *Don't splash!*" singing songs, "If you're happy and you know it, clap your hands." I could help with the little ones, but watching them makes me miss Meg, so I mostly just try to keep out from under the sweep of the counselors' enthusiasms and plot how to get home.

The third day I discover that if I don't mind a few scratches, which I don't, I can twist and haul myself branch over branch way up into a huge cedar tree at the back of the park. It's a relief to be alone. Now I can hunker down and order my thinking. I make a mental list.

One: I have to get back to Andersen Farm.

Two: Mrs. A. says Social Services is taking all the foster kids away from the farm.

Three: The A.'s are selling the farm because they can't afford to keep it if they don't have foster kids.

Four: If I don't fix the foster-kid problem, there won't be any farm to go back to.

Five: How am I going to do that? How's one lonely kid supposed to change the mind of the whole of Social Services?

Six: Why don't I just stay up here in this tree forever and starve to death, and years later they'll find my skeleton and then they'll be sorry but it'll be too late?

Seven: I can't let myself give up.

One: I have to get back to the farm. . . .

I'm not getting anywhere. I take a break and peer down through the branches at the campers playing their ninny games. Way over by the tennis courts I can see Garnet, fiddling with his cell phone. He's found himself a bit of privacy out of the counselors' line of sight. I can sympathize with that. Then two big boys I've never seen before come over and start talking to him. I know right away there's going to be trouble, because they're standing too close, and sure enough, it doesn't take them a minute before they start shoving him around.

Lines of loyalty drive me down to give him a hand. The farm taught me that—we might go at each other like sparrows and crows at home, but out in the world we stand together. That's why, even though we're all enrolled in the free-lunch program and dress mostly secondhand, no one at school dares mess with any of us Andersen kids.

I creep along behind a bush until I'm close to the three of them. By this time Garnet's on the ground. Now I realize how big these guys really are. They must be eighth-graders, at least. This is going to be different from hauling some angry six-year-old off little Meg, which I had to do a few times last year. I'd leave Garnet to his fate except for lines of loyalty.

"Get up," one of the bullies is saying.

"We didn't mean to knock you down," says the other. Garnet eases himself to his feet. "How about giving us that cell phone?" It isn't really a question. Garnet shakes his head and steps back. The first bully sticks his foot out, the second shoves him, and Garnet falls again. The big boys laugh. It sounds like something rusty scraping.

"Having trouble?" The second one reaches down. "I'll help you up. Just pass me that cell phone first."

I hold my breath. Can't Garnet see his only real chance is to give in?

"No," he says, sticking his chin out.

What an idiot!

The first bully lifts him upright by the front of his shirt. Now he's hanging from the bully's fists, the toes of his sneakers making little circles in the dust—and he's still holding on to that dumb phone.

Surprise is my only hope. I take a running jump and hurl myself against the bully's knees. Down he goes, and

I flump on top of him, flailing with my fists. Someone grabs me roughly from behind. Far away I hear Garnet yelling for help. Angry voices roar in my ears. I punch and kick wildly. I'm dead, but I'm going down fighting.

Then whistles blow, yells protest, feet scuffle. The bullies let me drop and tear away around the back of the tennis courts. It's over. The counselors troop us back to the community center and plunk us down in the office.

Of course, they want to know everything. It's not for me to blab out my own heroics, so I wait for Garnet to tell. He mouses his eyes around the floor and hums and haws and shrugs until Moira bursts in, crying, "What happened? Is everyone all right?" She races over to Garnet, who's only a tiny bit grimy, and begins flapping the dust off his pants. He pushes her away, I give him credit for that. When she's good and sure he hasn't broken any bones, she takes a look at me and gasps.

I know exactly why. She just spent all day Sunday throwing out my old clothes and buying me new ones. I let her do it because it's nice to wear something first-hand for a change. I was thinking how impressed the kids at the farm will be when I go back with all fancy new clothes. I only protested twice. Once was when she tried to throw out Jess's heirloom skate shirt, which he gave me specially to remember him by. She called it a "filthy thing." Sure, maybe it is a bit smelly, but it's covered with the signatures of real professional skateboarders that Jess collected himself at Slam City Jam. You don't wash a shirt like that. Moira and I bargained that I could keep it if I promised not to wear it.

The other thing I wouldn't let her do was cut my hair. No chance of that! My hair is my strength and my vanity. Mr. A. calls the color "wheat straw." Mrs. A. says it's "corn silk." I'm never cutting it. It's way past my shoulders now. Underneath, at the back there's a nice, nesty lump, which is comforting to feel when I tilt my chin up and is convenient to keep pencils in. I comb the top layer over it as smooth as I can, so it's not messy or anything. My bangs are long for hiding my thoughts behind. No one touches my hair but me.

Now my nice new T-shirt has nosebleed stains all down the front of it, and the pocket's ripped off my shorts. Even the gleaming snow-white leather high-tops I promised her I'd keep clean forever are scuffed and dusty.

Then it's "What happened? What happened?" all over again. This time Garnet talks. "I was just showing these guys how my cell phone works and Gemma comes along and starts fighting them. I don't know why."

I almost jump out of my chair and give him a bloody nose of his own, but then I think: "Wait! Kids have private reasons that are more important than what they tell grownups. I'll hold off and ask him when we get home." So I make myself count thousands, and when they ask me for my version, I just narrow my eyes and shrug.

Moira herds us off to the van. The head counselor follows us outside, and I hear him tell her that tomorrow the whole camp is going on a year-end picnic to the beach and they don't want to take me because they can't trust me to behave. "But I have to be in court tomorrow," she cries. "What'll I do with her?"

The counselors put their heads together and decide that I can stay in the office with someone called Sandy.

Moira thanks them over and over, and we head off. Garnet climbs in front, leaving me to sit by myself in the back. I don't care. I just want to get home and hear how come he said what he said. My experience is when you've fought for someone, it makes a kind of glue between you.

I wouldn't mind that.

seven

Once we're inside the house, Garnet heads for the second floor. I'm right on his heels. At the top of the stairs he breaks into a run. For a little guy he's fast. Too bad for him—so am I.

He dodges into his bedroom and almost gets the door shut, but I jam it open with my foot. "Hey, Garnet."

"What do you want?" He asks it through the crack, not friendly at all. This is starting off wrong.

"What was all that about?"

"What?"

"You know what!"

He moves the slice of his face that I can see right up to the crack. "I never asked for your help."

"Yeah, but you needed it."

"Get this straight, stupid. I don't need you. For anything. I don't want you."

I'm not expecting that. Salt stings up behind my eyes. I blink hard and tighten my throat.

He's not finished. "If you hadn't come here to live, I could've stayed home by myself this week. We were only at that ridiculous camp because Mom and Dad didn't want to leave you on your own. You're just a bunch of trouble. No one wants you. No one."

I'm gulping for air. "That's not true."

"No one in the whole wide world!"

"Not true, not true, not true!"

"Name someone. One person."

"Ruby! Ruby loved me."

"Ha!"

"More than you." I've got him now. "She gave you away. She kept me."

"Mom and Dad *chose* me, stupid. Ruby didn't care. She kept you because she was stuck with you, that's all."

My voice is rising. "She loved me. She took me camping."

"Camping! That's a laugh." His scorn stabs me back, and he slams the door in my face.

I'm halfway up the attic stairs when an explosion of fury blows away my thousands. I race back to his door and kick it so hard it shudders. "She did so!" I yell. "And she sang to me. She loved me!"

"Gemma!" Moira comes rushing down the hall. "Gemma, you stop that!" I bolt for my room.

Camping was Jess's idea. I was in second grade. We'd just spent all day making Mother's Day presents and discussing what was special about our moms, and these girls kept whispering that I didn't have a real mom. By the time I got on the school bus home I was feeling pretty ragged, and then someone looked at me sideways and I burst into tears. Everyone was sniggering because only sissies cry on the school bus. Then Jess came and sat beside me and asked me what was wrong. When I'd sobbed out my story, he asked if I could remember anything about my mom, and I told him my one thing. "I was sitting on her lap. We were someplace dark and small. She was rocking me and singing."

Right away he said, "I bet you were in a tent." The whole rest of the ride home and all the long walk up the driveway he told me stories about my mom taking me camping, how good she was at catching fish, and how she could name the stars. As soon as he said it, I knew it was true.

Ever since then, that memory's been my most precious possession, more than my books, even more than Pippi Longstocking. Ever since then, my most tender, secret, safest place inside is when I imagine camping with my mom. It's the one single thing I allow myself to think about her. And Garnet would wreck it if he could.

By the time I reach my room, I'm raging. I tear around, throwing myself against my screen walls. One after the other they twist and tilt and clatter over. Out of the corner of my eye I can see Moira at the head of the stairs. Let her try and stop me. I storm a wild dance and yell and yell. Then I throw myself on the bed and wind myself in the blankets.

". . . when your Uncle Dave gets home," I hear her say. When I finally look up, she's gone.

My head is just about shattered. I have to concentrate as hard as I ever have, ever in my life, to stop my memories of Ruby from shredding away. *Think, think, think.* And then suddenly I burst through and I'm there, at the edge of the lake. My mom and I are coming out from swimming. My little body is all goose bumps. My mom pulls off my suit and hugs me in a towel. Then she carries me into the warm, dark tent and cradles me and sings sweetly into my ear.

Now that I'm safe in my dream again, rocking in my mom's arms, I need to consider what to do next.

One: I have to get out of here.

Two: I have to fix the problem of the farm.

Three: How will I do that?

I wish I knew magic. Sorcery didn't work the other day, but that was because I'd never practiced it before. Spells take years of study—everyone knows that. I need something fast. Maybe there are shortcuts for people who only want to bewitch one thing. The library is right next door to the community center. Maybe I can do some research there tomorrow. This bolsters me up. I'm always heartened when I think of a plan.

On the farm, if any of us go to our rooms for a fit and we don't hurt anyone and we don't break anyone's stuff and we clean up after, we don't get into trouble. But of course we never knock down the walls, either. At the farm we have real walls. Anyway, I don't know what it's like here, and I don't want to get hit, so I hop up and get busy with the screens.

Standing them upright is harder than I thought. When Dave arrives, I'm still struggling with the first one. I back well out of his arm's reach in case he has a temper, but he tells me right away he doesn't want to be enemies. Then he lays down the law about fighting, and how there will be peace among us in the house. It seems they've decided I must have attacked the bullies because I wanted to join in some kind of game they were playing with Garnet. "You and your brother will get along together in no time," he says. "And you'll make lots of friends at school." I nod and nod, because what's the point of arguing? They're going to be on Garnet's side; it only stands to reason. Those are their lines of loyalty. And anyway, what do I care about them and their fake psychologizing? They can think whatever they like. I'm going home.

He helps me wrestle the screens back into place. "I don't know how Moira put these up by herself," he says. "She doesn't look it, but she's terribly strong."

We go downstairs, and he makes me apologize to Moira. I even have to shake Garnet's hand, which is total phoniness. No one who tries to mess me up with my mom gets a second chance. No one. He's my enemy, inside and out. I'll never have lines of loyalty for him.

eight

It's deepest night in our safe, warm tent. I'm snuggled in the sleeping bag next to my mom. I reach out to touch her silky hair. My hands scrape on something rough and cold. "Mom?" She rolls over. Bog breath. Slime and scales. It's not my mom. It's Red Boy. His eyes pop open, and he grabs me. "Where's my mom?" I cry. He roars a laugh. "Your mom's gone, and now I've got you!" The tent walls zigzag open, spin away, crash down. I struggle and kick, but I can't get free. He lifts me up and opens his mouth. Fire drips from his rolling tongue.

I manage to muffle the screams I wake with before Moira and Dave hear. There's no point in calling for help from people who don't know how to hold you. Red Boy nightmares never came so often on the farm. *Please, please, please let me find a way to get home.*

Next morning Moira drives us to day camp and deposits me with Sandy, a lanky man with pimply skin who turns out to be the summer-camp accountant.

"I don't want any trouble," he tells me. "I've got a lot of work to do today." We watch as the picnic bus carries the rest of the campers merrily away. "Frankly, I have no idea what to do with you." His eyes, teeny-weeny as minnows, dart resentment at me from behind the thick panes of his glasses.

"I could go to the library."

He brightens up. "That's an idea! You can hang around the office till it opens, I guess."

The secretary arrives with a box of doughnuts. Sandy eats two chocolate ones and brightens up even more. He sits on her desk and starts to tell jokes. This gives me courage and I ask him if I can phone the farm. I've been longing to call all week. I asked Moira once, and her face pruned up like she'd smelled something rotten and she said, "Perhaps it's not a good idea to bother them." *Bother* them? I started to breathe hard through my nose and beat thousands out on my leg, and she said okay I could. But she stood right there while I was punching in the numbers, so I hung up before anyone answered and told her the line was busy. Did she think I could talk with her busybodying over me like a bird of prey?

Sandy says I can use the phone if it's not long-distance and shows me into an empty office.

Right away I tell Mrs. A. about my nightmares. "Two! I've had two already! Once I wet the bed!" She sends her best hugs, but what can she do? Mr. A. is feeding the horses. The kids are all out somewhere. "Can I talk to Pippi?"

"Gemma! Try to see the bright side. Of all my kids, you're the lucky one. You aren't with strangers. You have a real family who want to take you in."

"You're my real family," I wail.

"We would be if we could, but we can't. You know that. Be brave, sweetheart. We love you. Here's Allan."

Mr. A.'s voice, dark and sweet, comes through the line. "Keep the faith, baby." He's always saying that. I want to tell him about my bad nights, but my mouth is numb. "Keep the faith," he says again. "Promise me?"

I force the words out. "I promise."

I hear the click as he hangs up, and then I have to rest my forehead on the cool of the desk and wonder how I can feel so heavy and so empty at the same time.

At ten o'clock sharp I'm the first one at the reference desk. The librarian smiles when I ask her for sorcery books and leads me off toward the children's area.

"I don't want children's," I tell her. "I want the real thing."

Maybe I look overly desperate because she stiffens up and asks me where my parents are. I back away, waving vaguely toward the computers. I can tell she'd like to stick with me and make sure I'm being looked after, but an old man waylays her to complain about how someone's done the crossword in the morning paper again, and I make my escape.

Safely out of her sight, I hunker down to think. I don't really need her help. I'm a whiz at research. I got the top mark in my school for library studies last year. Not that the competition was all that tough. "The Classification of Invertebrates" wasn't a popular topic.

There's a long line of people waiting for an Internet connection, and the truth is, I'm not too experienced with search engines except on the school computer, so I decide to stick with books. I look up "Sorcery" in Title Keyword and head over to the stacks to browse around call number 133.

I find seven likely candidates and arrange them on a table in order of hopefulness. All morning I read and read. I find spells for losing weight, curing cancer, finding love, winning the lottery, unearthing buried treasure, commanding the spirits of the dead, and torturing your enemies. There are spells for healing and damning and blessing. There's even one for creating your own vampire servant. But there's nothing for making Social Services change its mind about closing down a farm for foster kids.

By the time Sandy comes to fetch me for lunch, I'm feeling pretty discouraged. He invites me for a swim, but I tell him no. I've got to find a way to fix things, and I'm not going to find it at the swimming pool.

There are only two books left to look at. The first one is written by a truly terrifying couple who stare out from the cover with smiles so hypnotic and sinister I have to turn the book face-down for fear of falling under their evil spell. I open the second and bump into a forest of long, hard words. "Teleology." "Empirical."

"Demographic." I run to look them up in the big dictionary by the reference desk, but even when I know the definitions, it's hard to understand what they mean. And they come so thick and so fast that the librarian starts to take notice. I don't want her to ask me again about my parents, so I decide to plow forward on my own. "Pragmatism." "Deontology." "Dissertation." It's no good, I'm lost. Now all that's left is the book with the scary authors. Magic is dangerous enough. "Magick," which is how they spell it in the title, is probably worse. If I open the book will I be in their power?

I can see people lounging in a reading area by the windows, so I wander over there to have a little rest and gather my courage. The only free chair has a small book resting on it. I pick it up and flop myself down.

It's a funny thing about me and books. I can't resist them. Even though my eyes are scratchy from reading all morning, my fingers automatically start flipping through the pages.

A story flies out. It pours in through my eyes as if it has wings and my heart is its nest. The minute I read it, I know how to solve my life. The library around me goes fuzzy and golden. A ray of sun floods through the window and glazes the page with holy light. I hardly dare breathe. A miracle is streaming down around me. How do I keep hold of it? I start to read the story again, slowly this time, to etch each precious word on my brain, when Garnet and Sandy bound around the corner of the stacks.

"Here you are!" Sandy says. "We've been looking all over." As if I were deliberately hiding.

"Mom's waiting in the van," Garnet adds. "You'd better hurry."

All I can think is, I can't let go of this book. "I need to get a library card."

"She's double-parked. And she's cranky." As if it's my fault. "Come on!"

What can I do? My hand slips the book under my T-shirt, and I follow the two of them toward the exit.

When I hit security, the alarm goes off and the gate locks. I panic and try to jump over. My shoelace catches on the bar, and I pitch to the ground. I try to shuck out of my shoe, but it's a high-top, so I hang there upside down for what seems an eternity before I can wrench myself free. Then quick as lightning I'm up and bolting for the door. Garnet's too stupid to get out of my way; we tussle, and then Sandy catches hold of my hair. I'm done. He plucks the book from where it's sliding out from under my T-shirt and returns it triumphantly to the ring of library staff who've gathered to watch. He's still holding on to my hair as he marches me to the van.

Moira takes one look at us, collapses over the steering wheel, and buries her face in her hands. I knock on her window. "It's okay," I yell through the glass. "I know how to fix everything."

Her shoulders heave. I can't tell if she's laughing or crying.

nine

I fly up the stairs to my room. Maybe I don't have the book, but I'm pretty good at remembering what I read. I know how the story goes even though I don't have the exact words. I just have to go over it in my mind to keep it there.

"Once upon a time, long ago, there was a servant girl. She worked for a rich, cruel man. He yelled at her all the time, and he beat her, too, often for no reason. One day it was spring. She wanted to see the wild flowers, so she sneaked out to the meadow. She thought she'd be only a minute, but the afternoon flew by. All of sudden, she realized it was dinnertime, and she hadn't even begun her chores. She ran home as fast as she could. She was crying because she knew her master would skin her alive. But when she got back—a miracle! The house was sparkling clean, dinner was in the oven, and—lo and behold!—there was an angel in the kitchen, making the bread."

It's the happiest and most hopeful story I've ever

heard. Now I know exactly what I need to fix my life—an angel. Angels have powers. Bright, good powers. An angel could fix it with Social Services so the farm stays open. He'd fly right up there to the Social Services building, and with a flick of a feather he'd make all those government people see how cruel it is to break up a happy home. They'd realize a farm is a good, healthy environment for children to grow up in, and they'd get on the phone right away and tell the Andersens they've changed their minds and to keep up the good work.

An angel could fix it so I could go back to the farm and stay there safely forever. He could explain to Dave and Moira that sure, it's nice and fancy at your place, but it's not Gemma's *home*, and you're nice enough people, but you're not *her* people, and they'd understand and ask humbly if they could visit, and I would consider it. Those things would be pieces of cake for an angel. It's way better than sorcery, because having an angel means that someone who loves you is watching over you, and taking care of you, and you don't have to worry about fixing things all by yourself.

What's my first step? All I can think is, I need to find that book again. It will have clues at least.

Someone says, "Knock, knock." It's Dave, and my curtain door flops around from the pretend blows of his knuckles. I know why he's come. It's because of how that book got stuck in my T-shirt at the library.

I haven't worked out what excuse I'm going to give, but I have to say "Come in," so I do.

Dave isn't looking forward to whatever's coming next any more than I am. I can tell because he stalls around my room fingering my books and then peers for a long time at Jess's skate shirt, which I've thumbtacked like a power shield to the ceiling that slants over my bed. I tell him how Jess gave it to me when I had to leave the farm, and I point out the signatures of the professional skaters. He seems interested, so I unpin it from my wall and show him the back.

I don't know anything about skateboarding—just what I overheard Jess and Darren saying—but I seize the opportunity to stave off the lecture I know I'm going to get. "This is Kevin Hurley, and he can do a triple alley-oop backside flip, and this is Izaiah Mad Boy York. He's famous for doing a switch-heel shove off a ten-foot wall." I'm just getting wound up into a mode of bright enthusiasm making all this up when Dave drifts over to my desk chair and sits staring into his cupped hands. I'm in for it now. I sit down on the bed and hug the shirt to my chest for courage.

When he finally asks me for an explanation, the worst thing about it is how tragically sad his floppy eyes are. I fight the feeling that I've let him down—because what happened at the library is basically his fault. I want to tell him, "Look, I'll be out of your life in no time at all. I'm figuring something out which will make it better for all of us. I'll be rid of you, and you'll be rid of me." But then I'd have to explain about getting an angel, and I'd never reveal such a tender thing to anyone, except maybe Jess.

Thinking about Jess this way makes me horribly sad, and I crumple up around the pain in my chest. This has the unexpected effect of making Dave think I'm sorry about the book, and that gets his sympathy up, so my weak little "It was a mistake" is all he needs to let me off the hook.

"Gemma," he says. "You need to understand that if you want something, you just have to ask. If it's reasonable, we'll do what we can to help you get it. The world is not a hostile place. You are not alone."

I have to stop myself from jumping up and yelling in his face that he doesn't know squat about the world, and what's he talking about—he'll give me what I want—when *he* was the one who came out to the farm in the first place and exploded my life and took me away from everything I ever knew and ever loved? "One thousand one, one thousand two . . ." I'm getting a headache from clenching my jaw so hard, and when he finally goes, I bury my head in my pillow and scream silent screams until my throat is sore.

The next morning Dave announces that we're all going on a hike up in the North Shore mountains. At first I'm greatly resentful not to be able to dash to the library and find my book. Then I get to thinking that this mountain expedition might not be a totally bad thing. I'm not a thief, but the one time I *was* caught stealing, I never went back to that store again out of sheer embarrassment. I don't have that choice with the library, so it might be smart to give the staff a couple of days to forget my face.

After breakfast, the house erupts into fussing, with Moira packing lunch and directing the rest of us where to find the cooler and the water bottles and how to fill them up and fetch mosquito repellent and gather hats and sunglasses and extra sweaters. Then she insists that we put on sunblock before we leave the house because, she says, it take twenty minutes to start being effective and mountain air is thin. She actually puts it on Garnet herself, like he was six. One look from me and she hands over the bottle. I never heard of thin air except in the stratosphere, but I don't feel like an argument. Then she has us wipe our hands on a towel so we don't get everything greasy. *Fuss, fuss, fuss.*

I've been in the van with Moira and Garnet all week, but this morning, when Dave's there, too, my legs balk like a colt's at the thought of getting in with all these same folks who scooped me up from the farm. The only thing that keeps me from bolting is the image of myself chained to a bed. Besides, I know how to solve this if I can lie low long enough to get it organized. I grit my teeth and hold my breath as the van door rolls shut and cages me in with my keepers.

On the way up the freeway the Burdettes play a complicated game of Spot the Volkswagen, where they subtract points for PT Cruisers and multiply the score by different amounts depending on the speed limit and the color of something I don't quite catch. They try to explain the rules, but I don't have the heart to pay attention.

We don't go out much all together at the farm. Mr. and Mrs. A. are usually too busy to take time off. But when we do, for a birthday or something, and we go out for burgers, it's so much fun. We play Volkswagen Punch and Smart-Car Slap, and it can get pretty rowdy. We sing "Wheels on the Bus" for Meg or whatever baby we've got at the time, and Mr. A. knows all these ancient songs like "You Can't Always Get What You Want" and "Oh, Lord, Won't You Buy Me a Mercedes-Benz?" and "Give Peace a Chance," and we sing those, too. When we pull out of parking lots, we always roll down the window and sing "Born to be wi-hi-hild" at the top of our lungs. Once we sang it into the drive-in intercom at the Dairy Queen until the manager came out and Mrs. A. had to apologize.

Now I cram myself against the van window and sing "I'll Sing You One-O" under my breath to keep the blues at bay.

We park at the foot of the mountain and take a gondola up to the base of the ski hill. It swings us backward above the trees, up and up. I'm a little shaky on my feet when we get out because of how fast the city got small through the window. Dave tells me that at night the lights of the ski hill look like a question mark, and Garnet says, "Only sort of," and I say, "I saw it from my window," and Dave says he didn't know you could see it from our house, and Garnet says he always wanted his room to be in the attic, and Moira asks me if I've ever skied. I tell her no, and Dave says the whole family is going to Whistler Ski Resort for a week at Christmas and I can get started then. We start climbing.

First there are trees, and then there are shrubs, and then there's moss and lichen and rocks and a sky as vivid blue as a blank video screen. It's fine up here. The air is different. It *is* thin. Everything looks sharp and bright. I've never been up so high. In one direction I can see range after range of mountains, each one getting softer in the mist of distance until the last one melts away. In the other direction there's the city way down below in a blur of orange. When I get back to the farm, I'm going to tell everyone how neat the mountains are, and how we should come here, too.

I stretch my arms out wide. The wind blows past my ears like a long whoosh of angel breath. My T-shirt flaps against my sides like angel wings. The sky swirls a blue heaven around me. I feel a surge of knowing that everything is going to be all right.

ten

My new school is part of the same complex as the community center and the library. The seventh-grade classroom is in a trailer right next to the tennis courts where Garnet got bullied.

When we get there the first morning, Garnet hooks up right away with a boy who looks as wormy as he is. I hover uneasily on the edge of the room and watch the other kids comparing tans and telling summer stories. I've never had to face school without being part of the Andersen clan, and I feel unarmed and exposed. It won't be for long, though, and that's a comfort. I'll just keep my back covered, cooperate when I'm asked for something, and wear a bland face that won't draw attention or offend anyone. That should get me through.

Mr. Graham, our teacher, comes in and assigns our seats and gives us the usual first-day lecture about fulfilling our potential and respecting each other, and then he says that the library is our best friend and offers to issue a library card for any of us who don't have one already. And here's a stroke of good fortune that proves that fate is on my side: It turns out that the community library is also the school library, so the card that Mr. Graham puts into my eager hand is my open sesame to getting the angel book.

When class is dismissed, Garnet and I meet at the coat rack. Last night at dinner, Moira told us that in her opinion kids are being coddled too much by parents who drive them everywhere. "We're turning our children into lap dogs," she said. Then she said how nice it would be if Garnet walked me home for the first few days, until I got used to the way. It's only three blocks! And we drove it back and forth to that stupid camp twice every day all last week. I hardly need Garnet's help with that. Now we eyeball each other for less than a second before he flops off somewhere with his cell phone and I run to the library.

I motor past the checkout counter without looking left or right so as not to give any clerks who might remember me the chance to shoot me the evil eye, and head to the chair by the windows where I found the book last week. Of course it's not there. What was I thinking? I give myself a good punch in the leg for being so dumb. I do it harder than I mean to, and have to sit down to rub the pain away. *Ow, ow, ow.*

"Are you all right?" A hand touches my shoulder. It's the librarian. Her face is soft with concern.

Before I can stop myself, I'm blurting out my problem. "It's a little book." I make the size with my hands. "It's black. It has a story about how a girl gets an angel. I found it on this chair." Tears fill my eyes. *Sissy!* I blink them back. "It's about angels." I repeat that part clearly in case she's still worried about me and sorcery. She looks dubious. I fish my library card out of my back pocket and wave it at her. "I won't sneak it or anything."

"Well, that's all right, then, isn't it?"

"Can you help me?"

"You haven't given me much to go on. The call number for Religion is 292. We could browse the shelves." Of course! I should have thought of that myself. It takes her no time to find it. I feel like dancing a gladsome jig around her, but instead I seize her hand and pump it furiously. Then I run to the desk, check the book out, shove it in my backpack, and let my joy race me home.

When I open the door, a wash of piano music pours out from the living room. Garnet is practicing for some great recital. I feel kind of sorry for him because he has to get up early in the morning to practice, and he's supposed to get right back at it after school. According to Moira, he's some kind of prodigy. He has perfect pitch, she tells me, and an unerring sense of harmonics—whatever that means. He's playing at Diploma Level Two, which is terribly high for his age, and he got the highest marks last time and who knows what all else. She positively trills as she recounts his glories.

I'm starting up the stairs when Dulcie calls me from the kitchen. She's going to come over every afternoon to look after us until Moira and Dave get home from work.

"I'm making muffins," she says. "They're nearly ready."

I let the lovely, sweet smell of baking lure me in.

Petey's waiting for a visit. I'm pretty sure he knows me by now. Birds are smart. Pippi Longstocking, for instance, can count to twenty. The reason most people think birds are stupid is they don't do well on IQ tests. Imagine taking an exam from a giant a thousand times bigger than you are! You'd be way too scared to think. Why should a bird be any different?

I give Petey a little whistle. He edges close and chirps back. I wish I could let him out. He looks so sad in there. Maybe he'd like to ride around on my head.

"*Cheep, cheep,*" I say.

"*Cheep, cheep,*" he answers.

See how smart he is?

"Angels protect me!" Dulcie cries. "I've burned myself." The muffin tin clatters onto the cooling rack, and she runs to hold her arm under the cold water. "Close the oven door, will you, please, Gemma? And turn it off? Thanks."

"Does it hurt?" I ask.

"Not too badly." She shows me a red mark across her forearm. "I'll just cool it under here for a minute. Do you think you could tip those muffins out without burning yourself? Use the oven mitt."

"I've done this a lot," I tell her. "I help Mrs. A. all the time." Actually, Mrs. A. doesn't do much baking, but there's no big science to taking muffins out of a pan. These ones aren't as puffy as the ones that come from Costco. They smell better, though.

"Get yourself a glass of milk," Dulcie says, "and maybe you could see if there's an ice pack in the freezer."

The Burdettes' freezer is crammed with great stuff! There's a box of ice cream bars, a carton of rainbow sherbet, a tub of chocolate ripple, a frozen layer cake, two pies, and . . . "Look!" I hold it up so Dulcie can see. "Raspberry cheesecake! How about we have some of this?"

"How about an ice pack? And no cheesecake. We're having muffins." I finally root out an ice pack and help Dulcie tie it to her arm with a dishtowel. "That's enough excitement for one day," she says. "There's milk in the fridge and butter in the cupboard."

My muffin steams when I break it open, and the butter melts in. I lick it off my fingers. "Dulcie? Do you believe in angels?"

"Why ever are you asking that?"

"You said 'Angels protect me' when you burned yourself."

"Did I? Well, I don't know. My sister who lives in Alberta, now, there's no question in her mind. Once she was just about to cross the street when she felt a tap on her shoulder. She turned around to see who it was and a fully loaded gravel truck came barreling right through the red light. Missed her by inches. If she'd stepped off that curb, she would have been killed for sure."

"Who tapped her on the shoulder?"

"Nobody. That's the point. There wasn't anybody there. Frankie—that's my sister—swears up and down it was an angel."

This is an amazing story. My arms are all goose bumps. I pull my chair closer to Dulcie's. "So do you think a person could get an angel to help them if they really needed one?"

"The world is full of mysteries."

"So yes?"

"I guess so, yes. Do you want another muffin? They're good for you. They're full of ground flax. That's why they're just the teeniest bit flat."

"Okay." When I get back to the farm, I'm making muffins for everybody, and we're going to eat them with lots of dripping butter and glasses of cold milk. Muffins are better than frozen stuff any day when they're warm from somebody making them.

"Do you know," Dulcie says, tapping her finger pointedly on the edge of the table, "I've known Dave and Moira ever since they moved in here. I've known Garnet since he was a teeny little thing. I've watched him after school since the day he started kindergarten, and I never once burned my arm until they got that new stove."

I'm only half listening because there's something wrong with my insides. It's like a knife stabbing around in my guts. What's the matter with me? Am I allergic to ground flax? It takes me a minute to realize it's not the food, it's the piano. Garnet's given up on his beautiful, complicated sonata piece and now he's playing something horrible. The notes jerk and jar and knock against each other as if they're having a violent argument. It's ugly. It hurts my heart.

I push back from the table and run out into the living room. "Hey, cut that out!" His fingers tremble on the keys, but he keeps playing.

"Cut that out." I say it louder this time. He hesitates, then bends his head and starts all over again. *Clatter, bing, cring, crang.* Is he making it up or what? He's the great musical genius. Doesn't he know those notes don't go together? Even I know that music is meant to be pretty. It's not supposed to make you angry and sad.

I menace over him. "Do you hear me?" Now I'm yelling.

"Gemma!" Dulcie calls. "Come and finish your milk."

"He's not playing his practice pieces!" I know it's tattling, but I have to make him stop.

She corrals me back into the kitchen. "Leave him be," she says, and shuts the door behind us. "There'll be time enough to practice when his mother gets home." That's for sure. He wouldn't dare play that weird stuff with Moira around.

"I'll sing you one-o . . ." I sing it as loud as I can all the way up the stairs to drown him out. It's lucky I can't hear him from my room.

eleven

The book is called *Stories of the Saints*.

None of us farm kids ever go to church. The most religious thing we ever hear is Mr. A. saying drugs steal your soul, and telling us to keep the faith. But whenever we ask him, "Faith in what?" he only says, "Whatever gets you through the night." All I know about saints I learned from a girl who passed through the farm a long time ago.

Besides Jess and Arlie and Darren and me, and usually a little one like Meg, there are always other foster kids floating in and out who don't stick with us. One of them was a really weird teenager I had to share my room with when I was six or seven. Every night after lights out I'd watch her climb out of bed, kneel down, and whisper feverishly into her clasped hands. I asked her once who she was talking to. "God," she said. "I'm praying. Don't you know anything? What kind of a place is this?" I wanted to tell her, "It's a farm," but she really seemed frightened, and that made me frightened, too. I asked her if praying was the same as wishing very hard for something, and she said "No" so sharply I didn't ask more about it, even though I was curious.

She had a huge collection of playing cards with pictures of saints on the front and sayings on the back that she liked to memorize. There was one card with this almost naked man tied to a tree with I swear a hundred arrows sticking into his body and a ribbon of blood trickling down from every one. He was kind of arched back, with his eyes rolled up, like a dog when you pat its belly. I'd stare and stare and get this queer, watery feeling in my legs, because it was like he was enjoying being tied up with all those arrows digging in. I begged to see him every day, and she almost always let me. Then all the farm kids started playing Bloody Arrows and sticking each other with sticks, and Mr. A. locked up the cards. The girl left soon after that. I had no interest in the saints on the other cards, and I don't remember her saying much about them—just what special people they are, how rare and how blessed and all.

My story is near the back of the book, so I look there first. Sure enough, it's the last one, the story of Saint Zita. I read it thirstily. Then it sinks in that she was a *saint*, and my heart plunges. If you have to be a saint to get an angel, how will I ever get one? I'm not special or rare or blessed.

I read the story again and again, looking for clues, in the words, in between the words. Suddenly, I understand something important: Zita wasn't a saint when she got the angel. She was just an ordinary girl who got in trouble, the same as me. She must have gotten to be a saint somehow later, which I can find out easily by further research. My heart bursts happy again.

I pore through the rest of the book. It tells the stories of a hundred saints, arranged alphabetically from Abdon to Zita. I make a list: "Saints Who Got Angels." Not all of them did. When you're doing research, it's important to write good notes. Next day I buy a special notebook to keep them in.

I study the saint book every chance I get. At school Mr. Graham catches me reading it under my desk and confiscates it until the end of the day. After that I'm more careful, which slows me down. It takes me a week to comb through it thoroughly. When I'm done, I memorize my notes in case they get lost or burned or torn up by someone who's mad at me. Then I go back to the library and get more books. Every one of them has new stories, or at least new versions of the old ones.

I learn way more about my Zita. Whenever she got the chance, she took food to the poor. One day her master caught her sneaking out with her apron loaded with stolen bread. He demanded that she show him what she was carrying. When she opened her apron, out tumbled—not bread, but flowers! Another time, deep in a snowy winter, she gave her master's expensive fur coat to a beggar. The next day, when the coat turned up lost, her master raged around the house threatening doom on everyone. Zita was about to confess when a knock came at the door and there was an angel, returning the coat. And whenever she went out in the rain, angels would hold their wings over her head to keep her dry. They just couldn't seem to do enough for her. One other little detail: She lived in an attic, just like me.

I study my list of saints who had angels to figure out what they did to deserve them. Catherine Laboure swept up around the nunnery and cared for the chickens (chickens!), and angels showed her visions of heaven. Saint Julian the Hospitaler gave free food to wandering pilgrims. One day he fed an angel in disguise and got all his sins forgiven, which was a good thing since he'd accidentally killed both his mom and his dad. When Paris was under siege, Saint Genevieve ran the blockade and brought boatloads of wheat to feed the starving people. She had this lantern, and whenever the devil blew it out, an angel lit it again. Saint Agnes was tortured and condemned to death. Angels brought her a beautiful white raiment to wear to her execution. Saint Cecilia had such a lovely voice that angels gathered around to hear her sing.

I make another list. "Methods for Getting an Angel."
One: Be good like Catherine Laboure.
Two: Be generous like Julian the Hospitaler.
Three: Be brave like Saint Genevieve.
Four: Suffer like Saint Agnes.
Five: Sing like Saint Cecilia.
Four and five are out for me, because I sing the ques-

tion song all the time, and I'm suffering already from being away from home and missing my dear ones and worrying about the farm getting sold before I can fix things, and so far I haven't seen an iota of an angel. There's no point in even considering method three—I'm absolutely not brave. It doesn't count as bravery unless you're facing fear, and when I'm afraid, I run. That leaves me only method one and method two. I decide to try being good.

For a few days I make my shoes extra neat at the door, and hang my coat up evenly, and smooth my towel on the towel rack the persnickety way Moira prefers. She doesn't even notice. It's the same at school. I'm quiet and cooperative and don't read library books under my desk and hand my homework in on time, and what does Mr. Graham think? That it's the least I can do. Is that going to get an angel's attention? No, it's not. Generosity is my last and only chance.

I can be generous, no problem. Every Saturday morning Dave gives me an allowance of ten dollars, which is a fortune. At the farm we got chore money, but nothing like ten dollars all at one time. Except for buying a notebook for my angel research, I haven't spent a cent of it. Right now I've got $46.23. I count it every night.

Dave asked me if I wanted him to open a bank account for me. Apparently Garnet has a very impressive one. I told him no, and he said fine, it was my money and I could do whatever I wanted with it. I stash it under my mattress beside my mom's *Charlotte's Web* so I can float to sleep on my treasure-trove, loving the feeling of being rich. But I'd gladly give it away a hundred times over if it would get me an angel.

twelve

Saturday morning I wait for Dave to give me my allowance so I can be generous with the most possible money. Wouldn't you know, today he decides to sleep late? I wait and wait, passing the time by trying to tell Petey in cheeps and whistles all that I plan to do. If I were at the farm, I'd be telling Pippi Longstocking. She'd be settled nicely in my lap, and all the other chickens would be poking around eavesdropping and clucking advice.

Finally, Dave comes down rubbing his eyes and saying he thinks he might be getting a cold. All during his breakfast I hang around the table making my eyes big and looking needy. After his second cup of coffee he gets the idea and sends me for his wallet. As he pulls out two crisp, new five-dollar bills, he gives me his weekly speech on being responsible with money. "Don't spend it all in one place. A penny saved is a penny earned." Yes, yes, yes, I nod my head, my eyes glued to the cash.

The minute I get it I race to my room, dig my treasure out from under the mattress, fold the bills neatly around the coins, and wrap them in a plastic bag. There's plenty of people to give it to, all up and down Commercial Drive. I never saw such a thing out in the country, people begging in the streets, but now I pass them every day on the way to and from school.

Then I kneel by my bed, clasp my hands tight, and wish as hard as I can that this money will get me the good attention of an angel who will love me and fix my life. When I'm done, I shove the money into my sock in case of robbers, and go tell Moira I'm off to the library. She approves of the library.

It's chilly out this morning. I tuck my hands inside my jacket pockets. Some lucky person is going to be very happy with the warmth my money will buy. Who will it turn out to be? I walk blocks and blocks up Commercial Drive looking for that special someone. I see lots of poor people dozing in doorways, panhandling at corners, strumming guitars and singing tuneless songs for money, but none of them looks back at me with friendly eyes. I get all the way to the big intersection at First Avenue without finding anyone I dare approach.

I hesitate at the corner. Cars roar by, pedestrians push past. I don't know what to do. I could go to the bank and get all my money changed into coins and dribble them bit by bit into all the empty hats and guitar cases I pass. It's just that I'd imagined giving one special person the happiness of feeling really rich. . . . I'll have to keep looking.

I cross the Drive and start back on the other side. By now the tips of my fingers are numb with cold. The change has slipped down my sock and made a sharp bump under my foot that bites me every time I take a step. I can't very well stop to fix it here in the middle of the sidewalk with everyone walking by, so I hunch my collar against the cold and limp on. When I get to the library, I can drop into the washroom and do it there.

I'm cutting across the park when I see a woman standing in the middle of the empty wading pool. She's wearing a long skirt and rubber boots, and she's holding a plaid blanket around her shoulders with one bare, reddened hand. Her other arm reaches up, the cup of her hand open to the sky. She's standing still as stones. Dead leaves blow around her feet. I stop to see what she's doing.

Then I hear the high-pitched, insistent whistle of a chickadee. I look up and see him sitting on the branch of a nearby tree. The woman keeps her hand held high, not moving so much as a breath. At last he flies down onto her outstretched palm. In a minute, a second one comes, and then a third. I've hand-fed chickadees before, but never more than one at a time. How does she get them to stay there together? She seems to be talking to them. Then all at once they're done, and off they fly in a rush. She watches them go.

Sometimes in the lives of the saints there's a

moment when a sign of approval or direction comes zinging down from on high. For example, Saint Joan heard angel voices telling her to fight for France. Saint Theresa of Avila got stabbed by an angel's fiery spear when she prayed just the right amount. Saint Gemma Galgani's hands and feet would bleed without being cut whenever she did something specially good. What is this woman here but a sign for me? Who better to get my money than someone who loves birds the way I do?

The woman starts away, brushing seed husks from her hand. I hurry after her. "Excuse me," I call, but she doesn't hear. She takes such long strides that I have to race to catch up. What if I lose her? Daringly, desperately, I reach out and tug on her blanket.

She whirls around, clutching it to her chest. "What do you want?" The question cracks out. Her eyes are wild with suspicion and fear. I open my mouth, but words won't come. She peers closer. Her hair hangs in lank strings. The skin of her face stretches taut across sharp, sad bones. The smell of her is thick and sour-sweet. "What is it?"

I force the words out. "I wondered if you'd like to have this." I try to hold her gaze so she won't bolt as I unlace my shoe, pull off my sock, and shake out the plastic bag of money. She steps back warily. I hold it at arm's length, standing like a stone, the way she did for the birds. Finally, her hand darts out and snatches it. She carries it away a few steps, pores over it, and then looks up. "Is this for me?"

Before I can say yes, a thin, dark man with slicked-back hair flashes up beside her and dismisses me with barely a glance of his dead bullet eyes. Then he notices the money and a smooth grin splits his face. A slither of fear goes through me.

"Any more where that came from?" he asks.

"Oh, Dag," the woman chides him softly. Then she turns to me. "My name's Willow." She's braver now that he's here.

"I'm Gemma." Our hands touch. Her long, thin fingers are even colder than mine.

"Thank you," she says. Then Dag swings her around and leads her off toward a clump of people gathered under the overhang by the changing rooms.

I pull my shoe back on and run. I'm fizzing inside, bubbling, popping. My feet, my arms, my head, my heart are light as soda. Who could have imagined it would feel this good to give something away? I want to look after Willow forever, protect her, fatten her up, keep her warm. I'll come back here and give her my allowance every week! I only wish it could be more.

thirteen

Every Saturday morning after that, I take my allowance down to the park. I sneak some of Petey's birdseed, too, and Willow and I spend time with the birds. "That's Greedy Boy," she says one day, pointing out a purple-faced house finch sitting on a nearby branch. And sure enough, when we put out the seed, he's the first eager eater to arrive, and no other bird gets near until he's finished. "And that's White Face, his wife. See that patch behind her eye?"

"You have *names* for them?"

She shies away from my astonishment. "I suppose you think it's stupid."

"Oh, no! It's wonderful!" Willow is so smart.

Now she smiles when she sees me coming. Dag grins, too, a greedy gash that puts trembles in my knees. I wish he wasn't always hanging around, but she doesn't seem completely easy unless he's close by. He reminds me of a boy who passed through the farm once. He would protect us from outsiders on the school grounds, but he had this knife he liked to cut things with, and we had to give him our chore money. We clung around him the same way Willow does with Dag. It was scary to be his friend, but it was scarier not to be.

Every week I try to catch a moment when no one's around and call the farm. Every week the A.'s tell me it hasn't been sold yet, but no one ever mentions Social Services changing its mind. I add up what I've given to Willow so far. What I figure is that I'm probably being generous enough to hold off the sale but not generous enough to get an angel and fix everything once and for all. It's a worry.

Another worry is Petey, stuck in his cage all day, lonely and miserable. I'd like to buy him a little treat from the pet store, but I can't, because all my money goes to Willow.

"I'm sorry, Petey," I tell him. "Willow needs my help. At least you're warm and dry." I'm ashamed when I hear myself talking this way. I'm warm and dry, too, but the cage of this house is still a misery because it's not where I belong.

I ask Moira if maybe I could let Petey out for an afternoon. She looks at me as if I'd just sprouted horns. "Whatever for?"

It seems so obvious, I hardly know how to explain it. "He's in a cage all day. He's a bird."

"He was born in a cage. It's all he's ever known. Why would he want anything different?"

I sound out Dulcie one afternoon after school. "Do you ever think of letting Petey out of his cage?"

Her eyes pop wide. "Oh, dear me, no. That would be a disaster! He's never been out, you know. He wouldn't know what to do."

"He could fly around. . . ."

"He wouldn't feel safe. He wouldn't *be* safe. Don't even consider it."

"Birds are wild things. . . ."

"Even wild things need a safe nest, Gemma. You might as well think of freeing Garnet's fish. What would happen to them? They'd be dead in an hour. Goodness me!"

Then one Sunday, fate falls into my hands. In the middle of practicing, Garnet gets a stomachache so violent that Moira decides to take him to the emergency room. She says they'll probably have to wait hours. Dave is at a meeting. That leaves me and Petey all to ourselves. Now's my chance.

I watch from the front window until the van disappears up the street, and then I wait a bit longer in case they forget anything and come rushing back. At last I'm sure they're good and gone. The house looms large around me. It's the first time since I got here that they've left me on my own.

I tiptoe into the kitchen, even though there's no one to hear. "Petey, Petey, Petey," I call. He hops close, twittering hopefully. "How would you like an afternoon of freedom?" He cocks his head in a question. "You'll see."

I'm all fluttery inside. What an adventure he's about to have! Angels, look down and see me now.

I climb on a chair and lift the cage off its hook. It's surprisingly heavy, and almost slips out of my grasp. I have to hop around balancing it on my knee until I get a better grip. Petey's perch swings wildly. He tweets with the effort of staying on. I manage to get down off the chair without tipping it over, and carry the cage into the dining room. I start to put it on the table, and then I remember Moira's fuss over my simple fingerprint, so I set it on a chair instead. Good thinking! Petey and I are both relieved to have arrived.

My first concern is that Petey doesn't fly off somewhere and get hurt. A sparrow flew into the kitchen at the farm once, and Mrs. A. made us line up in front of the stove and wave our arms so it wouldn't fly too close and get burned. I swing the door to the kitchen closed and slide shut the ones between the living room and the hall. Then I make sure the windows are all locked tight. Petey would have no idea how to survive in the real world outside. Then I realize, What would happen if he decides to fly up the chimney? and pile a couple of sofa cushions across the fireplace. More good thinking!

When I'm absolutely sure everything is safe and secure, I open the door to the cage. "Ta-dah!" Petey preens his whole left wing before he even notices the cage is open and then takes a good long while before hopping over to investigate. Then he sits there for another long time, looking out at the unfamiliar room.

"Come along," I wheedle. I can't help worrying that time is passing. He has to be safely back in his cage before Moira and Garnet get home. "Come *on*, Petey." Finally, I figure maybe I'm crowding him by standing too eagerly close, so I back up and give him plenty of room. With a cheep and a chirp he hurls himself out.

At first it looks like he'll never get airborne, but he flaps his wings frantically and just before hitting the ground, up he goes. He makes it across the living room, reaches his feet out for the top of the curtains, misses, turns, flaps all the way back to the dining room window, veers away, and comes to a skidding crash-landing on the mantel over the fireplace. He blinks a few times, as though he's surprised himself by the wonder of it all. Then he takes a breath and flings himself into the air again. Around and around the ceiling he swoops, while I whoop for joy underneath. "Petey, Petey, Petey, come ride on my head!" But he's too happy trying out his new wings.

He finally comes to rest on the handle of the window overlooking the back yard. Now he can take his first real look at the beautiful wide world outside without the bars of a cage in the way. He opens his beak and sings. The notes carol up, higher and higher. His little tongue sticks out, his throat feathers vibrate. The room rings with his rejoicing.

A chickadee with a sunflower seed in its beak lands on a nearby tree. Petey pecks on the glass and sings again. The chickadee extracts the seed, eats it, wipes its beak on the branch, and flies off. Petey sings on and on. How can he sing for so long? How can such a little body hold so much breath? I curl up and listen to him tootle gloriously to the wind and the trees and the free birds flashing by. Seeing him enjoy his afternoon of freedom, I'm as happy as I've ever been helping Willow. Dear angels, please come and free me like I'm freeing this dear little bird.

The clock in the hall chimes one, two, three, four, five. Five o'clock already? How did that happen? I jump up. "Petey! Time to get back in your cage."

He doesn't seem to hear. His whole attention is glued to the darkening world outside. His breath makes a circle of fog on the glass. "I mean it, Petey." No response. I guess I'll have to put him back myself.

I go to get him, but he flies up from between my hands and lands on the curtain rod. This isn't working out. When Saint Francis told the birds to come, they came. What's wrong with Petey? I whistle and call, but he's too busy singing to take any notice. I jump and jump, but he's way out of my reach. I'll have to get something to persuade him down.

I grab a broom from the kitchen and sweep it across the curtain rod. He swoops down to the mantelpiece, but when I go to catch him there, he escapes to the top of the bookcase. I go after him again. Off he goes once more. This time he lands lower down, on the back of the sofa. I lunge for him, and he tumbles backward onto the floor between the sofa and the wall. I pull the sofa out, whip off my sweater, and fling it on top of him before he can scuttle away.

Now I've got him! I can't exactly see where he is, so I cram myself behind the sofa and gingerly pat the humps and bumps of my sweater until I feel him skidding around on the floor underneath. I hold him with one hand on top and reach under with the other. My fingers close on his little body. He's burning hot, and his heart batters furiously against my palm. He gives me a few halfhearted pecks, and struggles against my grasp. I kiss his head.

"Calm down, deary," I tell him. I'm not feeling so calm myself. I hear the van doors slamming outside and Moira's voice telling Garnet to hurry. I canter over to the cage, dump Petey in, and snap the door shut.

I'm on the chair trying to hang the cage back up when Moira and Garnet come in. "Why are all the doors closed?" she calls. "Who's moved the sofa? And what are the cushions doing in the fireplace?" Then she's in the kitchen honing in on Petey and me. "What's the matter with Petey?" He's on the floor of the cage, beak open, panting hard.

"I don't know." I finally get the hook attached and climb down. "I came to see. I was upstairs."

"Something must have startled him. Pretty bird, pretty bird." At the sound of her voice he begins to settle.

I race miserably up to my room. I wanted to do something nice for Petey, and all I did was nearly scare the life out of him. He's my only real friend in the house, but he probably hates me now. And Moira, who knows nothing whatever about birds, who thinks he's happy just because he's yellow—stupid, unfeeling Moira is the one who's calming him down. I throw myself on my bed and weep with shame.

At dinner I call down that I'm feeling sick. Then I bury my head in the pillow and sob myself to sleep.

fourteen

I'm a tiny bird in a castle room, fluttering frantically from place to place, looking for a way out. Below me, Red Boy whistles and thunders, knocking me this way and that with a broom. Then he throws something huge and heavy that knocks me to the ground. It's dark and I can't breathe. My heart pounds against my chest. His feet crash closer and closer. I know it's a dream, but I can't stop it. Now I'm Red Boy, stamping and stamping poor Petey with my huge, clumsy feet.

I gasp up through the surface of sleep and plunge into a waking nightmare of voices screaming guilt at me. Terrorist! Torturer! Bird abuser! I beg my conscience over and over to have mercy, but I know I don't deserve it. I betrayed my dearest little friend with pure selfishness. All I could think of was not getting caught for letting him out of his cage. I never for one minute considered how terrified he must have been with me chasing him all over.

I deserve to be punished. I want to be punished if only it will make my conscience stop. I've read of saints doing punishing things to themselves. Saint Peter of Alcantara slept with his head on a spike. Saint Mark cut off his own hand. I switch on my bedside lamp and reach for one of the saints books piled on my floor.

The first thing I read is how Saint Rose of Lima was so beautiful she couldn't get her good deeds done because of all the men crowding around. So she scratched her face raw and ugly with pepper and quicklime, and after that they left her alone.

I'm no beauty, that's for sure. There's no point in me rubbing pepper on my face. There's nothing I like about myself but my hair. I need it. I hide my true thoughts behind its wildness. It's my power. It's my beauty. I treasure my hair.

Suddenly, I realize a way I can punish myself good and proper. I kiss the Saint Rose page and slip out of bed.

Quietly as a cobweb, I creep downstairs and into the bathroom. The butterfly night-light casts just enough glow for me to find the nail scissors in the cupboard over the sink. I grab a hank of hair, put the scissors next to my scalp, and make my first cut.

There are a few things about this enterprise I didn't stop to consider. One is how much it hurts. This is because I have to pull my hair taut or else the scissors won't cut through it. Also, my arms start aching almost right away, and in no time I get a blister at the base of my thumb. This is good, I tell myself. The greater the pain, the more effective the punishment. Saints welcome pain. And then there's the sound. The tiny, blunt blades rasp through my hair like someone without a voice crying for help. I hum the question song under my breath to mute it from my mind.

Another thing is how long it takes. It's almost morning by the time I'm done. But the biggest shock comes last. Whose triangle face is that staring back at me from the mirror? Whose wide mouth, whose huge green eyes, whose stick-out ears? Except for the bare head with pickets of hair pronging up in random chunks, it could be Garnet's. At first I think it really is him, sneaking in to look over my shoulder. But it's not. It's me.

With a whimper of disgust I grab up swaths of my fallen hair, stuff them into the toilet, and flush. They don't seem to want to go down. I flush again. Water starts coming up over the rim of the bowl. I flush a third time. More water. I'm wadding the hair down with the handle of the plunger when I'm interrupted by a scream. I can't tell who it's from. Moira, Dave, and Garnet are all wedged in the door, staring open-mouthed at the new me, slithering around in my watery world.

Miss James, the therapist, sits back on the living room sofa and smiles. No one told me who she was. They all just crept discreetly out of the room with a "Here's Miss James, come to talk to you" as if leaving a kid alone with a total stranger were the most natural thing in the world. At first I think she's a social worker because she has a briefcase, but then she opens it and takes out a big box of tissues and I peg her for a therapist. Social workers don't bring tissues. They like to make you cry and watch you wipe your nose on your sleeve. Also, they don't smile. Miss James's eager grin is pasted all over her face. Jess says you have to watch what you tell any of these people. They're all from the government, and they all make trouble. I clamp my lips together.

"You can call me Lucy," she says. I glower and say nothing. "Do you know why I'm here?"

I bat my eyes innocently. "To fix the toilet?"

Her smile doesn't falter. She composes her hands in her lap. "You cut off your long hair."

I don't think it's necessary to comment on that. The evidence is pretty clear. Moira took me to the hairdresser's to get it evened out, which has left me almost completely bald. I look like a victim of war or chemotherapy. It created quite a sensation at school.

"Do you want to talk about why?" the therapist asks. I shake my head. I wish I had my bangs to hide behind. She leans forward. "Sometimes we do things like cutting off our hair because we have feelings we can't express in any other way."

In the kitchen Petey chirps feebly. I bite my lip. Silence stretches out.

Suddenly, Miss James pops to her feet. "Here's something fun we could do!" She drags two dining room chairs into the living room and turns them so they face each other. "You sit here." She pats one of the chairs. I comply as slowly as I dare. She plunks herself down on the other one. "Who would you like me to be?" she asks brightly. "Is there anyone you have issues with?"

Issues? I stare blankly.

"Are you angry with anyone? Do you miss anyone?"

"Pippi." The name confesses itself before I have a chance to stop it.

"Okay! I'll be Pippi, shall I?"

I wish with all my heart she *was* Pippi. "Okay."

"What would you like to tell her?"

"I miss you, Pippi." The words have a hard time getting past the lump in my throat.

"Now what would Pippi say to that?"

Pippi has the most special voice of any hen in the world. She's our pride and joy for recovering so well from the infection she had as a chick, but she did grow up with her beak a bit twisted over. She doesn't cluck. She almost purrs. I've tried to imitate the sound before, but it never comes out right.

"What would Pippi say?" Miss James insists.

I give it a try. *"Trrrrrruck. Trrrrrruck."*

"Trrrrrruck?" She hasn't got it nearly right. Pippi's voice is soft and sweet. Miss James's is sharp and blaming. *"Trrrrrruck?"*

I don't want to play this game anymore. Thinking about Pippi makes my chest want to explode with sadness. Pippi always comes when I call. I hunch over, wrap my arms tight around my knees, and concentrate on trying to look at the end of my nose. Silence stretches out again. The furnace comes on with a whoosh. I hear Miss James moving away and then a watery, inviting cascade of piano notes. She's running her hands easily over the keys. I look up.

"Would you like to play something?" she asks.

I'm tempted. She obviously doesn't know that no one but Garnet is allowed to touch the piano. She lets me take her place on the stool. "I don't know how."

"It doesn't matter. You can just make sounds. Experiment a little."

I play one tentative note with my index finger. After that I play another. Then I grow more brave and try a few combinations of two notes together. Some sound sweet. Some sound rough. The rough ones almost hurt to hear, but in a good way, like a nubbly facecloth in the shower, scrubbing out the sad places. I wish my fingers could move as surely as Garnet's. I find more pairs of notes that bristle together, and begin to experiment more boldly. I discover three notes that seem to like following each other. I go back over them so I won't forget, and then add a few more. It's fun. The harsh sounds ease the pressure in my chest. I'd never dare call it music, but once I'm used to it, my ears think it's pretty. I can hear in my head that the next notes should go up. I begin to search out the sound I want.

Suddenly, I realize what I'm playing. It's the exact same rough, scraping, jerky sort of thing that doubles me over when Garnet plays it. Miss James is smiling and nodding as if all this is proving her right about something and the joke's on me. Is it a trick to show I'm just like Garnet, or what? I'm an idiot! I slam the lid down so hard the keys ring, and storm out of the room. As I turn the corner of the stairs I hear Miss James calling, "Gemma? Gemma, what's wrong?"

fifteen

The Burdettes are careless with money. They leave
dollars and dollars lying all over the house. I'm always
passing little heaps of money, on countertops in the
kitchen, in the key dish in the foyer, on the table at the
head of the stairs. Dave comes home from work and
empties his pockets any old where. Moira likes to keep
convenient stashes for paying delivery people, and never
seems to think to put away the change. The Andersens
never leave such cruel temptation lying out in the open.
It would disappear into a kid's hungry pocket in an
instant. Nobody here even seems to notice it. *I* notice it.
I never touch it, but I count it with my eyes. One day I
count fifteen dollars, just lying around.

After I cut my hair, the weather seems suddenly colder.
Without my hair to protect me, the chill snakes down my
neck and nibbles my ears with freezing teeth. The days get
shorter and darker. I worry about Willow living out there
in the cold and the wet. Ten dollars a week seems pitifully

little help. I worry about not getting noticed by an angel. How long until someone comes and scoops up my beautiful farm? And there's all that money, just lying around.

One afternoon when I'm passing through the hall, my hand goes out all by itself and snags a small fistful of change from the key dish. Just at that exact moment, Moira pokes her head through the kitchen door.

"Gemma!" she says.

I stand rigid, the coins burning in my fist. "I was just . . . I mean, I didn't . . ." I can't think of what to say. I edge toward the key dish, hoping I can drop the coins back without her noticing.

Then she says, "It's pizza night tonight. Do you really have to have pineapple again this week?"

"No! No! Not at all." I'm so grateful that's all she wants, I'd be happy to give up pineapple for the rest of my life.

The next day I take a couple of quarters from the kitchen counter and a few more from the top of the piano. No one notices. By Saturday I have an extra five dollars for Willow.

When I get to the park, I find Willow and Dag and some of their friends huddling under a big orange tarp that they've strung from the changing rooms overhang to the branch of a nearby tree. I hunker down beside Willow.

She notices the extra money right away. "You got more," she says. She doesn't ask where I got it.

On the way home I try to be happy about Willow's tarp and the extra money I got her, but a question keeps slithering up that I don't want to have to answer. It has to do with stealing, which is something I don't do anymore. The last time I got caught they put me in an office with a real policeman who banged his fist on the table and threatened me with what happens to girls who get in the habit—reform school, jail, walking the streets. I promised him, and I promised Mr. and Mrs. A., and I promised myself I'd never do it again.

Does it count as stealing if you do it for other people? Saint Zita made the bread she gave to the poor, but she used her master's flour. Was that stealing? Saint Brigid gave so much of her father's stuff away that in the end he tried to sell her to the King of Leinster. When he turned his back, she gave his sword and robe to a passing leper. The king told her dad he didn't think he could afford her and sent her back home, but no one nowadays calls her a thief. If it wasn't stealing for Saint Zita or Saint Brigid, is it stealing for me? Will I get in trouble?

I'm in jail. Bars from a high window make stripes all over me. Chains weigh me down. From a desk way high above me, a judge looms furiously. "Guilty!" he bellows, "and your punishment . . ." The floor gapes open behind me. A blast of heat and a roar of flame rush out. The judge climbs over the desk. He pulls off his wig. He tears off his face. It's Red Boy. I can't run because of my chains. He lifts me high above the blazing pit.

I thrash myself awake in the lonely pitch of night. Where is comfort? If I were home on the farm, I could snuggle in with Meg or Arlie, or Mr. A. would hold me, or Mrs. A. would make me a cup of hot chocolate. Who can I turn to here? There's no comfort in this place.

I punch my pillow into a hen-sized lump and rock it on my lap. "I'll sing you one-o. . . ." It's no use. It's not Pippi, and the question song isn't working. I will explode into little pieces if I can't talk to someone who loves me.

I pull on my bathrobe and tiptoe down the attic stairs, along the hallway with its sleeping doors, and down into the kitchen. The clock on the stove reads 3:15. No time to be phoning anyone. I lift the receiver and punch in the number for the farm. Not to wake them up. Just to hear it ringing, and imagine the sound echoing through the kitchen, the hall, the living room, all the beloved places.

A whispery voice answers after the first ring. It's Jess! What's he doing up? Raiding the fridge? Lucky me!

"Hey, Gemma!" he says. "What's happening? It's the middle of the night."

"I had a bad dream."

"That's a bummer. Don't cry. A dream is only a dream."

"Can they put you in jail for stealing five dollars?"

"No one goes to jail for five dollars. Five dollars is nothing. You know that. What's bothering you?"

"I miss you."

"I miss you, too."

"How's Arlie?"

"Gone."

"Gone?"

"Last week."

"Where?"

"I don't know. Somewhere."

"Darren?"

"He was the first to go, after you. He ran back here, but they took him away again."

"Chained him up?"

"He only came back that one time."

"What can we do?"

"What do you think? Nothing."

I swallow back my tears. "So who's left?"

"Meg and me."

One summer Mr. A. took us to the beach. I stood at the edge of the sea and let the waves flap around my ankles. With every little lap and suck of water, the sand melted away under my feet. It was fun because when I got scared, all I had to do was run up to where the sand was dry. Standing here in the dark of the kitchen, I can feel my whole world dissolving out from under me. But there's no place dry to run.

"What about the farm?"

"Big drama last week. It nearly got sold. The real estate people were supposed to come over with the papers and everything, but all of a sudden the deal fell through."

"When?"

"Just a few days ago."

An inkling starts flashing in my brain. "When exactly?"

"I don't know. Tuesday, maybe."

"Not Wednesday?"

"Could have been. What's the difference?"

My hands are slippery on the receiver. "Jess, I did that. Me. I made the sale fall through. It's a sign."

"What?"

"Wednesday's pizza night. That's when I took the first money."

"Gemma, you shouldn't be taking things. Be careful, okay?"

"Do you believe me?"

"Sure, whatever. Listen, I've got to go. I'm not supposed to be up. You, neither, I'll bet."

"Don't worry, Jess. I'll save the farm. I promise."

"Keep the faith, baby."

"Bye, Jess."

Safe back in bed, I snug my blankets tight around me and think about angel power. It isn't mine to command yet, but the farm sale falling through is obviously a sign that I'm on the right track. Somewhere angels are noticing me. They're probably thinking, "Here's a girl worth helping. Let's watch and see what she does next."

What luxury not to be lonely. My angel is coming soon, I can feel it all the way to my toes. When my angel hugs me, will it be warm like human arms or cool like pillowy clouds? Will I hear its heart beating under my ear? Do angels even have hearts? Will it tell me it loves me best of all? Will it be a boy or a girl? I can hardly wait to find out. Be calm, be calm, I tell myself. Patience. For now, what I'm meant to understand is that taking money for Willow is the right thing to do. I have nothing to fear. That's enough to be going on with. I keep the faith.

sixteen

Now bad weather settles in with a vengeance. Day after night after day the rain pelts down. Fallen leaves clog the gutter gratings, and huge pools of water flood every street corner.

"We live in a rainforest," Dave says. "What can you expect?" Then he jokes that maybe he should build a Noah's ark in the back yard.

One afternoon on the way home from school, I see Willow running for a bus shelter. She's holding a newspaper over her head with one hand and clutching her raggedy blanket around her shoulders with the other. I run to catch up, and we sit on the bench together and catch our breaths.

"Where are you going?" I ask. She gives me such an empty look that I think she didn't hear me over the roaring hiss of car tires rushing through the puddles by the curb. I ask her again. "Where are you going?" She adjusts her blanket and peers out at the rain. It pours like a bead curtain off the roof of the shelter. I'm getting a sinking feeling about Willow and the rain. "Where do you sleep?" I ask.

She sighs deeply. "I'm looking for Dag. Have you seen him?"

A woman clutching a small girl by the hand ducks into the shelter with us. She flaps a shower of raindrops off her umbrella, and lifts the girl onto the seat. "There, there," she says. "The bus will be here in no time." Then she turns to me. "It's a filthy day—that's all you can say about it. A filthy, filthy day." By the time I look back, Willow is gone.

I'm at the house, trying to heap my coat on top of all the other coats that are piled on the hooks in the foyer, when it tumbles in on me about Willow. She hasn't anyplace to go. In this weather, no place to shelter. I know she's poor, and she hangs around under the tarp in the daytime, but I've never stopped to picture what she does at night. What was I thinking—an angel holds his wing over her? This is way worse than I thought.

In the kitchen Petey cheeps hello. I cut him a piece of apple and stick it through the bars of his cage. He hops over and pecks at it daintily. He seems to have forgotten his fear of me. I'm very grateful for that.

"Dear little bird." My voice finds a tune, and I work out a song for him and for Willow.

"Little creatures, trapped and trembling,
Winds cry high and rains fall low,

Winter weather, wet and heartless,
Makes the poor so lonely-o."

"Hey," comes a voice behind me. "That's my tune."
I spin around. Garnet is worming his way around the
door.

"What are you talking about?"

"Listen." He runs to the piano and plunks out the
same ugly, clashing string of notes that always makes
me so angry and sad. I'm just about to bang the kitchen
door shut when I hear, undeniably, under the jerk and
the jangle, the thread of the melody I've just been
singing. It's a different rhythm, but it's the same tune.

It takes me a second to recover myself. "So what if
it's your tune? Call the police, why don't you?"

"No. It's not that. I . . . I think it's great. Really I do."
His eyes are shining. "You heard my tune. You remem-
bered it."

"Aren't you supposed to be practicing for your concert or something?" I yell it right in his face.

"Now, now, now." Dulcie comes huffing in to break
us up. I raise my fist. Garnet retreats behind the piano
stool. Good. I don't like him. I don't want to sing his
stupid tune.

The front door slams. "Garnet!" Moira calls. "I don't
hear you practicing. The concert's four days away. Every
second counts. And Gemma, your coat's on the floor
again."

"There's no place to hang it. It keeps slipping off."

She puts her hands on her hips and gives it a long, critical look. "You're absolutely right. Let's take some of these things upstairs right this minute." She troops me up to the attic, both of us loaded down with armfuls of coats and jackets and hats and scarves.

We're hanging them on clothes racks when I get a thought so perfectly, absolutely, brilliantly right and good, and so obvious at the same time, I almost have to sit down to catch my breath. The Burdettes have way more clothes than they could ever, ever use. Why don't I take a jacket from one of the racks up here and give it to Willow? Who would ever notice? It's not as good as an angel's wing or having a home, but at least it will be something.

seventeen

"Don't spend it all in one place. A penny saved is a penny earned." I try to keep my impatient toes from wiggling my socks right off my feet as Dave fishes around in his wallet for my allowance. "Mony a mickle maks a muckle." There's a new one.

Garnet's practicing. I can hear some Beethoven thing through the kitchen door. He's been at it faithfully for the last four days—not a note of that goofy other stuff. The big concert is tonight. We're all going to hear him. Moira even bought me a new outfit, a floaty skirt, shiny shoes, and a fuzzy pink sweater with a spray of sparkles across the front. Imagine me in twinkly clothes!

"What do you do with all your money?" Dave asks.

"Stuff. . . . You know." I give him a glare to back him off what's not his business.

He throws up his hands. "That's fine. I told you, you can do whatever you want. I just wondered. Garnet never spends a cent. I was the same way. Save, save, save."

"What about my mom?"

"Your mom?"

"Ruby. Did she spend or save?"

"I don't know. I'm sorry, I don't remember." Finally, he hands over my allowance, and I run to put on my boots. I'm almost out the door when he calls, "What's in your backpack?"

I swing it around behind me. It's bulging fat as a sofa with the rain jacket and fleece I'm taking to Willow. "Books!" I say. "I'm going to the library."

"Funny about that," he says, coming down the hall, his big face bobbing like a friendly balloon. Why doesn't he go back and have another cup of coffee? "I heard a chiropractor on the radio just this morning. He said kids' backpacks are way too heavy these days."

"These books are light—really light." I bounce up and down in a careless kind of way. "See?"

He reaches out. "Let's feel."

I back away. "It's okay, really."

"He said a child's backpack shouldn't weigh more than ten percent of the child's own weight. You're tall, but you're pretty thin, Gemma. How about we go up to the bathroom and get on the scales? Just for curiosity's sake." I press myself hard against the wall. "You don't want to hurt your back, do you?"

I cower down onto the floor. This is all my fault. First I was just going to take the jacket. It's thin and folds small. Then I saw the lovely fleece and couldn't resist. I really had to squash it so it would fit into my backpack. I could hardly do up the zipper. Why didn't I see the danger? I'm an idiot. I shut my eyes and prepare for the worst.

Suddenly, there's a blast of buzzing from the smoke alarm in the kitchen. "Dave! Dave!" Moira's voice rings out shrill with panic. "Something got left in the oven, and the self-cleaner's on. I can't open the door. Come quick!" Dave races to the rescue. I scramble to my feet and flee.

Down at the park a whole collection of tarps and tents has sprung up under the trees by the changing rooms. People are sitting underneath their shelters, playing cards, chatting with each other, or just looking out at the weather. A mother is feeding a baby from a bottle. Some raggedy kids are splashing in the puddles. It's like a big family village.

I wander in and out looking for Willow. Then I hear her calling to me from a big old-fashioned canvas tent set at a distance from the others. Her face is plump with welcome. "Come in," she beckons. I duck through the entrance. Inside it's easily high enough for me to stand upright, and Willow only needs to stoop a little. There's no furniture. Bulging plastic garbage bags are piled two high against the walls. She pulls over a rolled-up sleeping bag, gestures me to sit, and gets a milk crate for herself.

"Isn't it nice?" she says. I don't answer because it makes me think about camping with my mom and my nose is prickling. Her face goes thin again. "Oh, well," she says and wrings her hands. "It's probably not fancy enough for you, but for me . . ."

"It's not that. It's very nice. I was thinking of a place I went once with my mom." Then I sneeze, which makes us both smile, and we sit companionably for a minute listening to the drizzle *tick, tick, tick* on the roof of the tent.

"It's sure a lot better to be dry than wet," she sighs. That reminds me why I came.

"Look what I got you." I pull out the jacket and fleece and hold them up for her to see. She doesn't reach for them, so I smooth them across her lap. "You can't tell the colors very well in this light, but I chose them specially for you. The fleece is red like rowan berries, and the jacket's leafy green. I thought you'd like them because on the farm the waxwings eat rowan berries all winter, and I know how you love birds. Do you want to try them on?"

"I don't think I should."

"Why not?"

"It's hard to keep nice things. . . ." Her voice peters out.

"But you have a place now. Now you can keep them."

Slowly she lets her blanket drop and pulls the fleece over her long, threadbare sweater. I help her roll up the cuffs. The jacket, too, almost drowns her skinny body. "You can wear layers under it," I tell her, "and it has a hood. It will keep the rain off, for sure."

"It has lots of zippers," she says. We count thirteen. I help her undo the ones under the arms so she won't get too hot. "It feels so light." She shrugs her shoulders up around her neck and caresses the soft fleece collar against the hollows of her cheeks. I'm so happy she likes it I hug myself. Suddenly, she says, "Do you want to see my baby?" Before I can even say yes, she's digging through the garbage bags. She finally comes up with what looks like a bundle of rags, which she cradles in her arms, cooing lovingly. Then she passes it to me and ever so carefully clears the wrappings away from its face. It's not a baby. It's not even a real doll. It's a chunk of smoothed-off firewood with eyes and mouth drawn on it with felt pen. It's creepy. I want to shove it away. But the longer I hold it, the more I see how artfully the rags are wrapped and bound. It almost has the feeling of holding Meg when she was small.

"Her name's Emily."

I don't know what to say. I've never met a grownup who still plays with dolls. I've never seen a doll as pathetic as this one.

"I know she's not fancy." Willow begins wringing her hands again. "But she's company. And like I say, it's hard to keep nice things." She takes it from me and tucks it away again, fussing until it's well buried. I can see her hands are trembling, and I'm afraid I've made her sorry she showed me such a tender, private thing.

Thinking to cheer her up, I pull out my allowance. "Which pocket would you like to keep it in?" I ask.

Before we can decide, we hear Dag's angry voice approaching.

Willow's face goes white. "You better go," she says. "Dag's not well this morning."

He gives me a dark look as we emerge through the flap of the tent. He's unshaven, and his hair hangs in greasy streaks over his forehead. "What's she doing in there?" he demands. Then he notices Willow's new jacket, and his eyes light up. "Where'd this come from?" He fingers the material. "You bring this?"

I nod, trying to edge past him.

"How about one for me, too?"

I'm stuck against the wall of the tent. "I don't know." I shove my allowance at him. It disappears into his pocket.

"Money's better anyway." Willow tries to step between us, but he grabs her arm and lifts her so she has to stand on tiptoe. "What with Christmas coming and all." He leers at me. "You know . . . presents." He spits the word.

"She does what she can," Willow says.

"I wish it were more, I really do."

"Stuff can get sold." He jerks his head toward the busy drive. "You know Cristo's New and Used?"

"The secondhand store on the corner?"

He nods. "Tell Mrs. Cristo, Dag sent you. She'll take care of you. You know what I mean?"

"Dag, please," Willow says.

"We understand each other, don't we, kid? We know

what it's like to really want something." I gasp a little, and triumph glints in his face as though he knows he's got me all figured out. I can't look away from his eyes. He's still holding Willow tiptoe in her boots, and now he's got me trapped.

"Leave her alone," Willow says.

He loosens his grip and lets her drop. "You leave *me* alone," he says, and stalks away.

Willow walks me to the edge of the park. She's rubbing her arm where he held it. Little rabbity tremors shudder through her body. I'm shaking, too.

"Dag's scary," I say. "I don't like him."

She puts her hand on my mouth and glances back over her shoulder. "Shh."

I pull her hand off. "He's mean. Look, he hurt you. Don't you see?"

She gives me a fierce push. "Go away," she says. "Mind your own business. Go away from here."

Now *I'm* the one grabbing her arm. "I'm sorry. Really I am. You're right, it's not my business."

She shakes me off. "You come here giving us stuff for whatever reasons, and all the time you're thinking, 'This is crap. These people don't know how to run their own lives.'" Her fingers are scrabbling to undo the jacket.

Now I'm sobbing. "It's not like that at all! You don't know. I go home where it's warm and dry and I think about you out here in the rain. Where I live there's so much stuff, and you have nothing."

"Nothing? You think I have nothing? That's what I mean. You have no respect. Why did you pick on me? What's in it for you?"

"I want to help. Please, please, please don't be angry."

"Keep your charity." She hurls the jacket down and strides away, wrestling the fleece off over her head. The jacket lies crumpled in the mud between us. I leave it there and run.

All the way home my feet pound questions at me. Do I disrespect Willow? Am I giving her things just for my own good? How could things have gone so terribly wrong? Where did I go off track? What can I do to make it better? When I get to the porch, I hunch on the top step and force myself to calm down. "One thousand one, one thousand two . . ." I can't go flapping into the house in this state or Moira will ban me from going to the library. Then I'd be a total prisoner. That's all I need.

It's been a terrible day. I screwed up with Willow. She didn't even get a jacket out of it. I almost got caught sneaking the darn thing out of the house. If it weren't for that stove accident happening at just the right moment . . . It was like a miracle. Then it hits me—it *was* a miracle! Exactly like when Saint Zita's bread turned to roses. I get goose bumps just thinking it. Angels must have been looking down and blessing me, too.

The glory of it nearly knocks me off the porch. No matter what happened afterward, no matter that Willow and I fought and she threw the jacket in the mud, no matter anything, angels are approving me. I can feel their power, electric in the air. I'll figure some way to make peace with Willow. I'll explain how I want to be her friend, not just because of getting an angel, but because I care for her—which is the honest, deep truth of it. Angels will help her understand. Angels will solve her life, too. Joy floods out of my throat. "I'll sing you one-o. . . . "

"You sound happy." Moira bustles past me into Dave's study. "Having a good day, are you?"

She has no idea.

eighteen

By the time we arrive at the theater for Garnet's concert, the lobby is crammed with people. Garnet slides off to wait somewhere backstage until his time to play, and Moira leads Dave and me and Dulcie, who's decked out in a dress even more sparkly than mine, through the crowd. Moira holds her face high and proud, smiling graciously from side to side. People stop her and ask about Garnet. They all mention how brilliant he is. She accepts their praise with noble silence while Dulcie clucks agreement, "Yes, he is, he's a brilliant boy. Always has been."

A woman asks, "Who's this tall pixie?" It takes me a minute to realize she means me.

"This is Garnet's sister." Moira gives me a little push forward. "Say hello, Gemma."

My voice comes out small. I'm not used to stares.

"And are you musical, too?"

Moira answers for me. "She's just come to us. She

hasn't had the advantage of a home where the arts are truly valued." I know what she means. She means the farm isn't good enough. I give her a fierce look, and her hand evaporates off my arm.

"She's still settling in," Dave says.

Soft chimes call us into the auditorium. Moira leads us down the aisle, nodding and waving to people she knows. I sit between Dulcie and Dave. He points out Garnet's name in the program. It's last on the list before intermission.

I take a look around. I've never seen such a grand room. Glittering chandeliers hang from a ceiling that's painted all over with cherubs and clouds. Above us sweeps a balcony with a golden railing. The air is buzzy with excited murmurings. For the first time I realize how important this night really is.

Dulcie says, "I don't know if I can bear the wait." She snaps open her purse and produces a box of chocolates. "Empty calories," she confides to me. "The only cure for anxiety. Take two, they're small." She passes the box to Dave.

By the time the lights dim and a hush falls over the audience, Dave and Dulcie and I have worked our way through the whole box. Moira just sits, getting stiffer and stiffer. A bald man in a black suit comes onto the stage and explains that tonight we're going to hear the cream of the entire Pacific Northwest's young musical talent. He says how hard all the performers have worked to get here.

"And I am especially pleased—no, honored—to be able to tell you," he says, jigging on his toes and rubbing his hands together, "that Sergae Obramavich, the conductor of the world-renowned UNESCO Youth Symphony Orchestra, is here with us tonight." A gasp rises up from the audience. "And he has graciously agreed to reflect on the performances he hears. This is a tremendous honor for us all." There's a burble of appreciation, and the bald man gestures outward. We all crane our necks to see a slight figure dipping bows from a private balcony near the back. Everyone claps enthusiastically. I see Dave squeezing Moira's hand. When we're finally settled again, the curtains whoosh apart to reveal a grand piano sitting by its lone self in the middle of an empty stage.

All the performers are way older than Garnet. All of them play like experts. With every new player, my stomach yanks itself into a tighter knot of nervous pain. I wish I hadn't eaten all that candy.

Garnet finally appears. He looks tiny as an ant crossing the wide stage. I count twenty steps before he gets to the piano. The boy who played just before him had long legs, and when Garnet sits, his feet don't reach the pedals. He tries to jig the bench forward while he's sitting on it, but he's too light, so he has to get up and shove it closer to the keyboard. My hands burst into sweat, and Dave rolls and unrolls the bottom of his tie.

I hold my breath. Finally, Garnet begins. He plays the first notes so sweetly I can almost hear the audience sigh. I settle back. Then all at once he stops. From where we're sitting I can see his hands reflected in the long mirror above the keyboard, his bitten-down fingernails. They hover uselessly above the keys, and then he lets them drop into his lap. Silence resounds. He sits motionless, staring down. Someone coughs. Still he sits. Moira leans forward, rigid as a rod, willing him to play. Dave wrings his tie. Dulcie squeezes my hand. I think I'll never breathe again.

After an ice age of time, Garnet straightens himself up and rubs his forehead with the back of his wrist. Then, using only one finger, he begins to pick out that tune of his, *doink, doink, doink,* in all its hesitating, broken-legged rhythm. When he gets through it, he plays it again, adding the terrible, teeth-rattling discords that give me the bends every time I hear them. The third time through I can hardly follow the tune at all. It's as if he's not interested in it anymore, but in something it makes him think of. Then he goes back to one finger single notes, slower and weaker, as if the poor, crippled soul of it were dying out. The notes fade away. Silence falls like a big wet blanket. No one claps. Not even Moira or Dulcie or Dave.

Garnet gets up and starts walking off. The tap of his shoes is the only sound in the place. Suddenly, I'm on my feet, frantically flapping and whapping my hands together, the sound echoing in the empty air. It's not for the music I'm clapping, that's for sure, but for his courage, playing that awful thing in front of all these people. Moira yanks me down and hisses furiously for mercy's sake to stop making a spectacle of myself.

The famous conductor praises everyone but Garnet. He doesn't even mention him by name. He says that we're only young once and we all learn from our mistakes, and that in this kind of situation it's best to stick to what we've practiced. Moira's face is a death mask. We don't go back after intermission.

No one says a word the whole drive home. When we get there, Dulcie says a quick good night and scurries next door. Once we get inside, I hurry to hang up my coat and escape to safety before Moira explodes. I don't make it. What did Garnet think he was doing? How will she hold her head up again? Didn't he know who was in the audience? Has he no respect? Couldn't he see what an opportunity . . . ? I start to ease myself out of the line of her fire when she zeroes in on me. "And you, Gemma, adding insult to injury by clapping like that. How could you?"

"But, but, but . . ." I want to explain that I didn't mean to, didn't plan to, wish I hadn't. I want to quench the grateful look that pours out of Garnet's eyes.

Dave puts up a silencing hand. "We all need to cool off. Garnet and Gemma, you go to bed. We'll talk about it in the morning." He puts his arms around Moira and folds her to his chest. She starts to cry. I creep away.

Garnet follows close on my heels. "Was that really you clapping?"

I turn on him and raise my fist. It wasn't my plan to

get in trouble for him and his stupid music. It's not my plan to have him glomming on to me for something I couldn't help. "Leave me alone, you creep."

I slam the attic door on his longing gaze.

nineteen

I'm venturing down to the bathroom next morning when I stumble over a folder that's been left on the bottom step of my attic stairs just inside the door. What's this? I carry it back to bed and open it up. It's drawings of . . . of . . . I flip through page after page . . . well, bones. Bones and skulls and teeth. All floating around on the page. Sometimes there's fish on the page, too, or weird animals, and sometimes streets and cars. Once there's a gun. But always, on every page, the most important thing is some kind of human-looking bone. I've never seen anything so creepy. Every page is signed in fancy, graffiti-style lettering, "by Garnet Burdette."

Why would he put these drawings on my stairs? Why would he want me to see them? He must have gone out of his mind after last night. Still, I'm not going to stomp on the revealing of a tender secret, no matter how disgusting it is. I grab a red marking pen and write "A+ work!" in my most teacherly hand across the front of the folder. On my way back to the bathroom I scrunch the edge of it under his door.

At breakfast Moira and Dave try to get me to explain why I clapped for Garnet last night. I can't think of a thing to tell them, so they banish me to the attic for the rest of the day. Garnet barricades himself in his room and refuses to come out. I can hear them through the floorboards begging and shouting at him.

Monday morning there's still no sign of him. I scuttle away to school, grateful to be out of the iceberg land of cold looks that greets me in the kitchen.

That afternoon Miss James, the two-chair therapist, arrives to see not me but Garnet. She emerges from her visit and secretes herself away with Dave and Moira. I try to get some idea of what she's saying by lurking around Dave's study door, but the voices are muffled, and I can't catch the words. Next day Moira sits silent as steel all through breakfast even though Garnet comes down, ready to go back to school.

Later that afternoon I have a snack with Dulcie. She's my best shot at finding out what's going on.

"It's quiet, isn't it?" I say, opening the topic. The house is almost eerie without the music of Garnet's playing.

"It certainly is," she says. We sip our milk and tea in silence for a moment or two and then Dulcie bursts out, "It's a dreadful thing. A truly dreadful thing."

"What?"

"Poor Garnet."

I try not to look too interested. "What about poor Garnet?"

She puts down her cup. "I suppose it won't do any harm for you to know. . . . The therapist told Dave and Moira that Garnet told her he couldn't stand the pressure of their expectations about his playing. He didn't want to practice all the time, no matter how good he might become, and he was sick with nerves thinking he might fail. She said he couldn't think of any other way to end it—except by doing what he did at the concert. 'It was a kind of breakdown,' she said. In her opinion, only time will tell if he'll ever touch the piano again. The poor child. Of course, it's very difficult for Dave and Moira to accept."

I'm glad I clapped for Garnet now, not because I like him any better, but because it serves Dave and Moira right for being so ignorant of his feelings. Mr. A. and Mrs. A. always talk to us about stuff. "Thanks for telling me," I say.

"That's all right," Dulcie says, and pats my hand. "Don't mention it to Dave and Moira if you can help it. I'm sure they wouldn't mind, but you know how it is."

"I know."

For the rest of the week the house stays in a freezing hush, and no one speaks to anyone else except to issue bare minimum instructions in a flat, dead voice. Garnet and I eat dinner alone in the kitchen with Moira crashing pans angrily by the stove. When there's trouble at the farm, there's a big blowup and then it's over. This long, cold grudge makes me sick inside. I throw up twice.

Finally, things begin to thaw, and Friday night we sit down to eat together for the first time since the night of the recital. Dave is hearty, and I can see he's trying to mend things. He praises the food and encourages us to take seconds. Moira's face has softened somewhat from the icy lines that have ribbed it since the disaster. She's making an effort, too. A thin smile hesitates on her lips, and she encourages it to bloom.

"How would the two of you like to go to *The Nutcracker* ballet?" she asks Garnet and me.

I've never seen ballet. I don't know if I'd like it. I wait to hear what Garnet says.

"That would be nice," he says in a quiet voice. I guess he can see he's being offered peace.

I'm grateful for it, too. "Should I wear my sparkly sweater?" I know how Moira likes to dress me up.

"Of course."

Then Dave says, "Speaking of Christmas, I trust you two have saved enough of your allowance to buy presents." Garnet nods. Dave beams, "Good lad," and turns to me. "What about you?"

Of course I haven't got a cent. I'll still get a few allowances before Christmas, but I have to save them for Willow. I haven't figured out quite yet how I'm going to get her to take them, seeing as how she's so mad at me. But as far as I'm concerned, they're hers, no matter what. Besides, it's Christmas for her, too. That's no time to cut anyone off. "Sure," I say. "I've got money." I don't know where I'm going to get it.

"That's good," he says.

"Christmas is coming so fast," Moira says. "The Salvation Army Santa Clauses are out already."

"I saw one this afternoon by the liquor store," Dave says. "And you wouldn't believe what else I saw—this man, begging for change, wearing a jacket exactly like my green one from Eagle Crest. A three-hundred-dollar Gore-Tex jacket! Where'd he get it? And he had the nerve to ask for change."

My mouth dries up, and my tongue turns to cardboard. I try a slug of milk. It goes down the wrong way, and I have to leave the table, milk dripping out my nose. By the time I've cleaned myself up, I'm furious. So somebody picked up that jacket? Good for him. Why shouldn't he? Doesn't he have a right to be dry? I only hope he got the fleece, too. How can Dave and Moira be so selfish? When did they ever have to run around in the rain with no place for shelter? They're way richer than they need to be. They deserve to have their stuff given away. "My green jacket from Eagle Crest," indeed.

Okay. That's it. I need money for Christmas presents, so I'll do what Dag said. I'll find something in the house and sell it at the secondhand store.

I come home right after school and comb through the attic. There's lots of stuff up here, but I need something they're sure not to miss, something small enough to sneak out without trouble. Not like that fleece. That was an error of judgment. I don't want Dave threatening to weigh my backpack again. A miracle saved me one time. Twice is too much to hope for.

I start out searching with high hopes, but everything is either too big or too awkward to carry out, like vases and tea sets, or dangerously valuable, like sterling silver serving spoons and pearl-handled knives, or just plain worthless, like family photos and out-of-date encyclopedias. After three days of hunting, I'm running out of places to look, and I'm close to despair.

The only place I haven't explored is a pile of boxes labeled "Christmas Decorations," stuffed way off in a corner. Who would pay money for somebody else's old ornaments? But now that I've looked everywhere else, I'm driven to desperate measures. I kneel down and start emptying cartons. First I unearth boxes and boxes of thick, expensive wrapping paper and ribbon, which under any other circumstances I could have pawed through for hours. I love beautiful paper, but I'm in no mood for it now. Then I get to the tree stuff—glass balls and bells, silver birds and stars, little carved wreaths and Santa Clauses, Play-Doh animals Garnet must have made in kindergarten. Most of it's fancier than we have at the farm, but basically it's just the same old Christmas junk that everybody stashes away from year to year.

I force myself to rake through everything anyway, my hands heavy with hopelessness. Nothing, nothing, nothing. Then at the bottom of the last carton my fingers close on something with a bit of weight to it. I pull it out.

It's an old wooden box with faded gold writing on the top. "Angel of Mons" it says. Angel! Here's a sign if ever I saw one. What does "Mons" mean? Monster? Monsoon? Some of the letters must have rubbed off, but I can't make out where. It doesn't matter.

Inside are little bundles of tissue paper. I take one apart and find a miniature soldier, very nicely made, and surprisingly heavy for its size. He's kneeling down with his gun across his lap. His head is bandaged. He's set on a little stand that has a fraction painted on the bottom: $\frac{15}{500}$.

I put him on the floor and peel the tissue off a second soldier. This one is running. I unwrap a dozen of them. Each one is different. One is lying down shooting his gun. One is standing up with his gun at his shoulder. One has a bicycle. One has a machine gun. All of them are in excellent shape, their uniforms shiny and their dot eyes gleaming.

I'm unwrapping the last one, thinking these little toys might actually be worth something, and suddenly, there in my own hands, nestled in petals of tissue, a true wonder reveals itself. It's the figure of an angel riding a horse. He's wearing white armor and holding a sword triumphantly over his head. His halo is shiny gold. I stand him on my hand. His long wings reach almost to my palm. A fizzing excitement bubbles up my arm. Yes,

yes, an angelic sign, sure enough. And it's telling me I'm meant to sell these soldiers. The more I think, the more right it seems. They're probably worth something for being old-fashioned, but they couldn't be very important, or else why would they be kept with all this worthless Christmas stuff? And they're small enough to sneak out easily.

I tuck them all back into the box, carry the box into my room, and slide it under my bed. I'll take them to the secondhand store on Saturday and get myself some Christmas money. All but the action figure of the angel. I'm not parting with that.

twenty

"Buying, selling, or looking?" A rough, metallic voice cracks through the gloom as soon as I push open the door of the secondhand store. I peer around. Who am I supposed to answer?

"Buying, selling, or looking?" the voice insists.

"Selling."

"What?"

"Soldiers." I offer the box to the empty air. "Dag sent me. He said to ask for Mrs. Cristo."

"Well, then, let's see." A beaded curtain at the back of the store rattles applause, and a great, gray woman shuffles through, her bedroom slippers hissing on the floor. A faded dress and loose sweater slop shapelessly over her body. Her hair is scraped back into thin, begrudging braids that wrap her head like wires. Her eyes are crow bright. "Just trying out some surveillance equipment," she cackles. "Works pretty good. I can see you. You can't see me."

She lifts the box from my hand and carries it over to the counter. In the fuzzy light from the dusty window she reads the writing on the top, "Angel of Mons." Her soft body comes alert. I want to ask her what the words mean, but she's already busy unwrapping the first soldier. When she turns it over and sees the fraction on the bottom of the stand, her breath goes in, short and sharp, and she gives a low whistle. I want to ask her what *that* means, too, but I can't take my eyes from her thumb with its long dirty nail caressing the numbers round and round. As she unwraps the others, her fingers begin to move faster, pulling greedily at the paper.

When all the soldiers are ranged together before her and the box is empty, she heaves a rumbling sigh and turns to me. Her eyes are dull and wary now. "Is there more? Anything else?"

"No." I say it to the floor.

"Are you sure? It's not worth much without"—she taps the blurry word on the lid of the box—"the angel."

"How much?" I hardly dare ask.

"I could give you fifty dollars."

"And with the angel? If I could find it, I mean?"

"Much more. It's a set, you see."

"How much?"

"Depending on the condition, maybe twice, three times as much."

A hundred and fifty dollars! What I couldn't do with that. But I'm not giving up my angel figurine for anything. "Can I have the fifty now?"

She takes a greasy change purse out of the pocket of her sweater and clicks it open. Then she pauses. "Let's have a little talk, shall we, missy? Where exactly did you get these soldiers? I can't afford any trouble."

I never anticipated she'd ask me that. I take a breath and start babbling.

"I got them at a yard sale in Langley? They were in a box with a lot of other stuff? Like hockey equipment? And the people I was with, they didn't want it? And now they're dead? And so the soldiers got to be mine?" I'm usually pretty good at spur-of-the-moment excuses, but the way Mrs. Cristo looks at me, I can't stop everything coming out like questions.

She leers down. "All right, all right. Here's your money."

I count the tattered bills. "But this is only thirty-five. You said fifty."

She bends close. A long white whisker curls from a mole on her upper lip. Her breath smells like throw-up. "Consider the difference a fee you pay for the . . . shall we say, 'care'? that I have to take in selling them. If you know what I mean."

I shove the money in my pocket and stumble out the door.

"Look for that angel—don't forget." Her laugh follows me onto the street.

I have to sit down on the curb until the bones in my legs come back. I'd planned to go to the park and try to persuade Willow to take this week's allowance, but I feel all sucked up and slimed, and I don't have the heart for it. I drag myself home instead.

***

Garnet waylays me at the door of his room.

"You want to slide?"

"Not really."

"I've been practicing. I can slide over halfway down the hall now."

"That's nothing."

"I suppose you can do better."

I scorn him with a look and walk back to the other end of the hall, breathing deeply, taking my time. Once I'm there, I shuck off my shoes, adjust my socks, and crouch down like a runner in the blocks, my back foot wedged firmly against the wall. Then I visualize how I want it to go while I rock back and forth, coiling and uncoiling my strength. When I'm perfectly focused, I blast up off the wall like a rocket. Three big steps and I start my slide.

When I get to Garnet's door I throw myself down like I'm sliding into second base, and at the end of the hall the soles of my feet slam against my door with drive to spare.

Moira's study door flies open and Moira rushes out. "What's going on? What's happening? Gemma, are you all right?"

"I'm fine." I get up perkily, but my hip is stinging.

"Garnet," she says, "you know you're not supposed to slide in the hall."

"She does it," he says, jutting his pointy chin at me. "All the time."

Moira turns her explaining voice on me. "We don't slide in this house."

"Why not? It's a great floor."

"Someone could get hurt."

"Kids mend," I tell her.

"No sliding," she says.

"That's just dumb."

"Gemma!"

"Kids aren't made of glass. That's the dumbest thing I ever heard."

"Go to your room this instant."

I make a lot of noise stomping up the attic stairs. I know Dave will make me apologize for being rude, but I don't care. Some of the rules around here are just too stupid.

That night I'm playing around with my angel action figure and I get this idea it might possibly be the image of a real angel. If it is, then it's probably going to turn out to be the one who's adopting me. Otherwise, why would it have been in that box of soldiers in the first place?

What can I remember from my reading? I was concentrating on saints, not angels. Besides, most of the angels in the stories didn't have names. There was Gabriel for the Virgin Mary and Raphael for Noah, and Uriel and Ariel for dreams and something else—but the one I remember best is Michael. He's the one who's going to smash the dragon Satan once and for all at the end of time. If he can do that, he'd surely have no problem with Red Boy. But really, dear angels looking down, I'd gladly take any one of you who wants to be mine, even if you're not famous. Please understand how much it doesn't matter as long as I get someone.

Now I'm worried. The more I think about it, the more sure I am that this angel figurine is a sign, and I'm not getting what it's telling me. If my angel sent it down to announce, "Here I am! This is me!" and I'm too dumb to understand, maybe he—or she—will lose interest and go on to someone smarter. I've got to do something fast.

I wait for Moira and Dave to call good night to Garnet and me and close their bedroom door. Then I wait at the top of my stairs, still as still, letting the house creak and sigh around me. When I'm sure everyone's asleep, I sneak downstairs to the kitchen computer.

I summon up a search engine and get millions of hits for "angels." Too many! I try "angels and horses" and get millions of hits for that, too. How do I decide where to begin? This is what I don't understand about the Internet. I chew a fingernail right down to where it hurts and get a brilliant idea—"Angel of Monster." Only one hit for that! It's a sign! I click on it and find an e-story about a girl called Jewel. Jewel! Hope flies up in me because of how close our names are. She's having an adventure in outer space. I read and read, scrolling down for what seems like endless hours, until finally in the last sentence she gets thrown in a dungeon by the Angel of Monster

Machines and then it's *dot, dot, dot,* to be continued. What does this have to do with my angel on horseback?

I get no hits for "Angel of Monsoon." "Angels on Horseback" is a recipe for broiling oysters and bacon. Ugh! I'm stumped for what to do next, so I go back to "angels and horses" and plunge in.

"Ya Like Angels? Horses? Pirates?" "Duck, Dolphin, Pig, and Angel Weathervanes!" "Angels on a Carousel!" "Angel Wallpaper!" "Angel Hair!" "Angel Eyes!" The screen screams invitations to buy, buy, buy. I'm lost in a gigantic supermall. My eyes start to sting. I'm getting nowhere, but I can't make myself quit. I feel like Jewel, lost in my own story that has no end. Will I just go on, *dot, dot, dot,* wandering in here forever? I lose track of what I'm looking for. I try to buy a lucky angel charm bracelet and some magic perfume, but you need a credit card for everything. Then I find some really gross stuff and I want to go to bed, but the hallway yawns like a big black mouth of evil possibilities and I don't dare leave the glow of the computer screen. I huddle up on the chair as best I can and doze until dawn gives me enough light to pad back upstairs to bed.

twenty-one

I wake what seems like only minutes later to the sound of the alarm. My eyes are gritty from too little sleep, but I force myself up. I have to get to the library to continue my research before my angel gives up on me. I tiptoe through the sleeping Sunday-morning house and let myself out the front door.

The library is dark and deserted. What's going on? I rattle the handle and pound on the door. What's wrong with this place? Just when I need it most . . . Then my cloudy mind connects it's Sunday at home with it's Sunday out here, and I check the schedule—which is posted right in front of my eyes—and see that today's library hours are one to five. Will my angel scorn me for being so stupid? Please don't, dear angel. I wish I had Pippi to worry with. I wish I had Jess.

I'm falling into a confusion of loneliness when I remember that one thing I could do now is look for Willow. I still have this week's allowance in my pocket.

I wander over to tent city, keeping an eye out for Dag.

There's no sign of Willow anywhere. I ask around, but nobody knows until finally this one woman with a kid in her arms gives me a nod to follow her out to the swings by the wading pool. "Willow's gone," she says.

"Where?"

"You're Willow's friend, right?" I nod. "You don't want to go blabbing this everywhere," she says, "but the other night Dag beat her up pretty bad. We took her to the emergency room and they sent her to a shelter." She fits her kid into a baby swing and rocks him gently.

"Can I go visit?"

"I guess so."

"Where is it?"

"Downtown East Side somewhere. Go to the Carnegie Center—Main and Hastings. Ask any woman down there for the Powell Street Women's Shelter. They'll tell you where it is."

I'm at the house and heading back to my room when I meet Garnet in the hall.

"You liked my drawings," he says.

I push past him. I don't want to talk to Garnet about his drawings now. I want to think about Willow.

"I did another one. Want to see? Wait, I'll get it." I head up the attic stairs. He calls after me. "I'll bring it, okay?"

Poor Willow. I hope she's all right. That Dag! I'd like to punch his ugly face. I give my pillow a couple of good belts, and I'm really getting into it when Garnet worms through my curtain.

"You okay?" he asks.

I dump the pillow on the floor and grind it under my heels. Feathers start to come out. Now I feel better. I kick it under the bed and flop down.

Garnet waits until my breath slows before he ventures closer. He holds out his picture. This one's very elaborate, some kind of hanging structure and a lot of people digging. And bones, of course. "What do you think?" he asks. "I got some images off the Internet. It's a collage."

"What is it about you and bones?"

"It's how they find people. Teeth, dental records, like that."

"What people?"

"Missing people. You know—people who go missing in your life."

I don't know what he's talking about, but it's making me queasy. "Listen, Garnet, I think you're a really good artist and everything, but I'm not feeling so great right now. I'd like to be by myself, okay?"

"What's wrong?"

"Nothing's wrong. Just give me some space, okay?"

"You can have my drawing if you like."

"No thanks."

"I might be an archaeologist when I grow up."

"See you later, Garnet."

"You're right about sliding. There's nothing wrong with it."

"Go away."

Finally, he gets the hint and takes himself off.

At one o'clock on the dot I'm back at the library, buzzing over to the reference desk. The librarian is still getting herself settled at her desk.

"I want to know what angels look like," I tell her.

"Goodness! Well." She seems a bit flummoxed. "Nobody really knows for sure—that's the problem. Lots of people think they don't really exist. They're sort of a metaphor."

"They do, too, exist."

"If you say so." She shakes her head doubtfully and straightens some papers, as though she's giving herself time to think. Then her face brightens. "I can find you pictures of angels. I can't promise you that's what they really look like."

"I don't want made-up angels. I need a *real* one. Riding a horse."

"A horse?"

"A horse!"

She puts her hands up to calm me. "Let's just take a look on the Internet, shall we?"

I hang over her shoulder while she searches.

"Don't go there. It's scary." I point to *"XXX. Wild Angels Ride."*

"No, of course not. Did you . . . ?"

"Not really."

"You poor kid. Stay away from anything that's

labeled 'XXX,' all right?" I give the back of her chair an impatient little shove. "That's enough of that," she says sternly, but she lets me urge her on and turns back to the screen.

We can't find so much as a feather of a real angel riding on a horse. "Now what?"

"Gemma, if you'll let me sit up straight . . ."

I give her a bit of room. "Now what?"

"We'll try books. Let's go to the fine-arts section and see what we can find." We set off to the 704s together and she leaves me there with a big pile of art books to look through.

I hunt for a long time, through volumes and volumes of the most amazing old paintings. I find angels swirling through the skies and lazing around on clouds. I find them singing carols and blowing trumpets and strumming harps. I find them carrying ladders and scolding sinners and weeping and laughing and, over and over again, giving lilies to the Virgin Mary. They're praying, mourning, dancing, fighting. But not one is riding a horse.

I get teary because what can I conclude from all this except that my angel action figure isn't a real angel at all? I go blubbering to the librarian, and she comes right away to help. She ignores all the big, impressive pictures that had grabbed my attention and concentrates on small black-and-white ones scattered throughout the texts. In what seems like no time, she finds a small blurry photo of a stove tile from a castle in Czechoslovakia.

And there it is—an angel riding a horse, stabbing a dragon with a long spear. He's wearing armor and he has a halo, and his long wings reach down almost to the ground, just like my angel figurine. And underneath the picture, right there in black and white, it says, "The Archangel Michael killing a dragon."

There it is, plain as day. Now I know. My special angel *is* Michael, my number-one choice. And he's not just any ordinary angel, either. He's an *archangel*. I look it up. It means he's a chief! I'm as good as home free. I float back to the house on a cloud of goodwill.

twenty-two

As we drive downtown to *The Nutcracker* that night, I imagine myself leaping cloudy chasms on the back of Michael's horse. His angel arm is tight around me so I won't fall. I look down, down through the feathers of his wings at the tiny world beneath us. Way, way below I can see the farm coming into view and Jess and Arlie and everyone running out to wave. I settle into my seat in the theater thinking about how everything is going to work out perfectly for Willow and for me now that Michael's on our side. Then the curtains glide back, and I'm swept into another glory.

Every step, every leap, every twirling pirouette the dancers make send surges through my body. My muscles imagine themselves stretching and soaring and bending and spinning. My chest fills with the joy of it. At the end, everyone is clapping, and when the people around me get to their feet, I stand with them and clap harder, and Moira doesn't mind because she's clapping, too.

On the way out my legs itch to jump and prance. In the press of the crowd funneling through the exit doors I keep myself reined in, but as soon as we get free on the sidewalk, I can't help letting go. I jump up onto the ledge of one of the courtyard fountains and balance there with tiny, dainty steps. Moira rises to her toes and does a perfect ballet sweep with her arms. Our eyes meet, two *Nutcracker* dancers, and then I take a great Sugarplum Fairy leap off my perch, and slither all over on my slippy shoes, and Dave has to catch me before I tumble into an old couple hurrying by. Clumsy me! Still, I know something about ballet dancing now: it's a kind of flying, soaring and majestic, graceful and wild, like riding Michael's horse will be.

We find the van in the underground parking lot and wait in a long line of chugging cars to get out. Dave yawns broadly. Moira asks how we enjoyed the show.

Garnet says he liked the giant mouse. "The battle would have been better if there'd been blood, though."

"Garnet!" Moira exclaims.

"It wouldn't have to be real. It could be . . . red glitter or something. Remember we saw that clown in the circus who threw a bucket of water at us and it turned out to be popcorn? That's what I would have had. Buckets of glitter blood. *Buckets* of it."

I don't have words to say how much I loved it. My face feels like it's breaking with happiness. Moira smiles at me so kindly I think for a moment that she wishes she could dance, too.

Finally, we reach the street, and Dave swings the van left across traffic.

"Where are you going?" Moira asks.

"Hastings Street."

"Not through the Downtown East Side."

"It's much faster this time of night."

"Dave!"

"It'll be all right."

"Are the doors locked?" I hear the click of the automatic lock. Moira peers around her headrest. "Are your windows good and closed? Are your seat belts done up?"

What's the problem? I press my face against the glass. There's not much to see. It's dark out there and beginning to rain. Tippy, tippy, my toes dance on the floor of the car. When I get back to the farm, I'm telling Pippi Longstocking all about *The Nutcracker*. I'll tell her how my legs and arms danced along with the dancers even though I wasn't moving. She'll be amazed.

"Lord almighty," Dave says. "Another red light." His fingers drum impatiently on the steering wheel.

"I don't see why you think this is faster," Moira says. A shadowy figure waving a squeegee plunges out from the corner and weaves in front of the van. Moira flaps her hands at him and mouths "Go away!" A wet cloth splashes across the windshield. Dave blasts the horn. The figure disappears.

"What the blue blazes is the matter with the wipers?" Dave's voice is rising. "The windshield fluid's empty. Who—?"

"Dave! The light's green."

"The windshield's all smeared. I can't see a thing."

"It's fine, Dave."

"No, it's not fine."

"For heaven's sake!"

"I have to pull over."

"Just drive home. We can wash the windshield there."

He swings the van over to the curb. "Is there some Windex under the seat?"

"I'm telling you, let's go home."

"Moira!"

She fishes up the Windex, and he climbs out of the van and starts to clean the windshield with his hankie. The man with the squeegee comes back. He and Dave wave their arms and shout at each other.

I put my fingers in my ears because my stomach is already queasy from Dave and Moira arguing, and I'll throw up if I hear any more fighting. Then I notice that my right arm is glowing red, and the watery smears on the windshield are streaking like blood. I peer out my window. Feverish light boils down. Nightmare smashes in.

There in the black sky above me is Red Boy, eyes blazing, mouth gaping, scales flashing gory red and green. I pull off my seat belt and scrabble at the lock beside me. I can't get it open, so I scramble into the front seat and heave myself against the driver's door. The handle pinches my fingers, and I can hear myself whimpering. This is no dream.

"Gemma? What's wrong?" Moira reaches for me, but I swing the door open, throw myself out, and run.

The sidewalk is dark, and the flames from Red Boy's mouth flash crimson in the puddles ahead of me. I'm pelting into a lake of fire. I don't care. I can hear him snapping and twisting at my heels. I have to get away. Halfway up the block I skid on my slippy shoes and fall. Hands grab me. It's Dave. I punch and kick and scream about the danger, but he won't listen and I can't wrestle free. I scream and scream, but he won't let me go. Why can't he understand?

A siren whoops. Piercing lights jitter red, blue, red, blue. A police car mounts the curb in front of us and lurches to a stop on the sidewalk. Two policemen pile out and demand to know what's going on.

"It's all right, officers," Dave gasps, struggling to keep hold of me.

"I'll have to see your ID," one of them says.

"Can't you see . . ." Dave begins. I wrench myself out of his grasp, but I'm off balance and in two steps I'm caught again. This time it's a policeman, and there's no getting away because his arms lock me tight against his body. I bury my head in his jacket and wait for Red Boy's jaws to clamp down. They don't. I hear Dave telling the other policeman, "I'm her uncle," and then Moira's voice, high and hysterical, "I knew something like this would happen if we stopped. All of a sudden, she just jumped out of the van."

"Is he your uncle?" my policeman asks.

I open my eyes. Dave has his arms around Moira. They're not fighting anymore. I begin to relax. "Sort of."

"Sort of?"

"Her mother was my adopted sister," Dave says.

"So he *is* your uncle."

"Sort of."

"He's her uncle," says the other policeman.

"Can you tell us what happened?" mine asks.

I can't say Red Boy's name out loud. "I just got really scared. There was this man with a squeegee . . ."

"It's pretty scary down here," he agrees. "You folks really shouldn't be here at all. It can be dangerous."

"I told him," Moira begins.

"Yes, you did," Dave agrees. "You were right."

"You'd all better take yourselves off home now," the other policeman says.

"I'm not going back there," I tell them.

"I'll get the van," Dave says. He jogs down to retrieve it, and we climb in.

The whole drive home no one asks me anything. Everyone seems perfectly content to believe that the sight of a man with a squeegee would make a twelve-year-old girl flee for her life. I feel awful for blaming it on him. I hope he doesn't get in trouble for it. I hope the Archangel Michael can see into my heart and know the desperation at the bottom of my lie. I shut my eyes and wish fervently for him to come soon and deliver me from Red Boy once and for all.

twenty-three

I wake to the blur of day, my pink attic room cloudy around me. Through the fringe of my lashes I see Moira sitting in my beanbag chair, tapping away on her laptop. What's she doing here?

She sees me waking and comes over. "How are you feeling?" Her hand is cool on my forehead.

"Fine." I sit up. Actually, I'm feeling a bit shaky. "What time is it?"

"Eleven. We thought we'd let you sleep in. You had quite a night last night." She helps me on with my bathrobe. "Come on down, and I'll get you some breakfast."

She makes me French toast, which is only ever for Sundays, and lets me have all the maple syrup I want. I feel like I could drink glassfuls of it. When I'm done, she sends me up to dress and then piles me into the van. I assume she's taking me to school, but she drives right past.

"Where are we going?"

She glances over but doesn't answer. I start to panic and consider jumping out at the next stoplight, but I'm still scared of Red Boy. I know it couldn't have been real last night, but if it wasn't, I don't know what it was.

Moira drives downtown to a place called the Goh Ballet and Modern Dance Academy. "Here we are," she says brightly, and I follow her up three flights of wide stairs. Slender boys and girls in leotards and tights, sweaters draped with careless grace around their necks or their waists, lean against the walls, chatting to each other and laughing quietly.

"How come they're not in school?" I ask.

"They go to school *here*," Moira says. Her voice is a reverent whisper.

At the top of the stairs we take off our boots and go into a huge empty room with a gleaming blond floor and two walls of windows and two walls made entirely of mirrors. We look like alien invaders standing there in our heavy coats on the edge of the shiny floor. A door opens on the far side of the room, and a fairy steps through. She's wearing a blue leotard and tights, with a filmy little skirt on top. Her feet are bare. Her hair is pulled back into a sleek bun, and her eyes are mountain sky blue. She moves toward us as smoothly and gracefully as if she were floating. When she smiles at me, I flow toward her like a rivulet into the sea. Moira tells me she'll be back in an hour and leaves us. I hardly notice her going.

"Would you like to dance with me?" the fairy asks. Her voice is like bells.

I start to say, "Oh, no, I can't dance," but the words don't come, and my head nods yes. She slips me out of my coat.

"See if you can follow me." She starts to wave her arms in that floaty way, and I do, too. Pretty soon we're gliding up and down the lovely long floor, twiddling our fingers and feeling the air rush between them. My arms are so soft I feel like crying, and I sneeze, and then I stomp my feet to put a stop to that, and the fairy does, too. We stamp, and pound, and growl, and pounce. We run and run. I'm the leader now. When I tumble, she tumbles. When I take a run at sliding, she slides after me, and I see how she doubles her leg under so she doesn't crunch on her bones. I can do it, too! The wilder I get, the wilder she gets, and all the while her sky eyes sparkle with mine. Then it's like nobody's leading, we're in a wild rumpus together, howling, and barking, and sometimes laughing, and sometimes terrifying ourselves with our fierceness. Then we flee, and flee and scare ourselves more, and curl up like bugs until our insect legs rebel. Then we kick ourselves upright and fly, and flee, and jump, and roar some more.

Moira finds us heaped together against the wall, too tired even to talk. When we leave, the fairy takes my face in her hands and kisses me on the forehead. It tingles like a star.

On the way home Moira asks me if I'd like to go there again.

"Oh, yes, please!"

Over the next couple of weeks Moira takes me back quite a few times. One time the blue fairy and I make up a dance about the farm. I show her how I run in the wind in the fields "Yah! Yah!" and we experiment with how to make shapes for the fragrances of horses and hay. She's been in *The Nutcracker*, and another day she teaches me steps from one of the children's dances. Another time I'm worried about Willow, and we cower under our blankets and feed flocks and flocks of birds. Sometimes when we're looking for ideas, we find them in scary places, like nightmares. She's afraid of hearing an old-fashioned clock strike thirteen. We sing *"Bong, bong, bong"* and crumple our bodies and cower and cringe as the numbers rise, and when thirteen comes, we scream and change into swans and escape on long white wings. I tell her bits about Red Boy, though I never say his name, and we spend almost the whole of one visit crawling on our bellies in imaginary mud while Red Boy roars and stomps above us.

One evening after that, Dave calls the family into the living room. He and Moira settle on the sofa, and Garnet grabs a cushion and throws himself down by the crackling fire. I sense an ambush, so I perch on the arm of a chair near the door. Dave gestures with his eyes for me to settle closer. When I don't, he clears his throat and says, "We've been trying to understand what happened to you the night of *The Nutcracker*, Gemma."

Ambush. I was right. I tense up, ready to jump. If he

asks me one single thing, I'm leaving. I'm not talking about it, and he can't make me.

But he doesn't even try. He just hands me a photograph.

It's a nighttime picture of an empty city street and a building with a neon sign in the shape of a seahorse hanging off the side of it. Underneath, neon letters say ONLY SEAFOOD CAFÉ. The picture's entirely dark except for the glow cast by the pink and green threads of light that outline the name and the little animal. Its dainty mouth is shut. Its tail curls shyly. It has no teeth, or arms, or legs. It floats airily above the street, like a friendly cartoon figure. It's nothing to be afraid of, but my heart chills at the sight of it. I hand the picture quickly back to Dave.

Garnet peers at it, and says excitedly, "That's where we stopped the van, right? Where the squeegee guy was, and Gemma freaked out?"

Dave goes over and drops the picture into the fireplace. I watch the little seahorse and the dark street below it bubble and flame and curl into ash. He takes the fire tongs and very deliberately knocks the ash to powder. Then he says, "We've been talking with the therapist."

"What therapist?" I ask.

"At the dance academy," Moira says.

"The blue fairy? She's a *therapist*? All we do is dance around and play imagination games." Suddenly, I've got this feeling of being pried into and peered at. I start edging away.

"Sit down, Gemma," Dave says, in a voice that makes me do it. "Listen for just a minute. We've been talking to the therapist, and we've been piecing things together, and this is what we imagine might have happened to you the other night."

I look longingly out at the safety of the dark front hall, but Dave tells me again, "Listen! This is important." I make a wall with a silent "I'll sing you one-o," and his voice goes small. "We think that when you were little, when you were still with Ruby, the two of you might have lived somewhere near that seahorse sign. If something way back then frightened you in that place, seeing the sign the other night could have reminded you of it. When that happens, when old memories are triggered like that, things we've forgotten can come rushing into our minds in a frightening way. But, Gemma, listen to me: There's nothing to be afraid of now. Do you understand? Nothing. Whatever it was, it's over."

Is that where Red Boy came from—a neon sign over a restaurant? Is this the end of Red Boy, ashes in the fireplace? No more nightmares? Please, oh, please, let it be true.

"Is that where Ruby lived? Somewhere around there?" Garnet asks. "Do we know the address?"

"No, Garnet, we don't," Dave says.

"Can we find out?"

Dave shakes his head. "There's no way. Landlords down there don't keep records."

"I just thought . . ."

"Not now, Garnet."

"We were worried about you, Gemma," Moira says softly. "We care for you, and we want you to be all right."

"And one other thing," Dave says. "I am your uncle. Really. Not just sort of."

The fire is warm on my face. I concentrate on how the flames leap and play. We watch until they flicker down, and then we watch the embers roll and die. No one says anything, which is a good thing because I'm in a storm of feelings, and I'm holding myself from breaking apart, and one word would do it. Dave's wrong about being my uncle. I don't get what's so important to him about making me his niece. He doesn't know a thing about me, and he never asks. Why is he so greedy to break me apart from the farm? He doesn't know a thing about love and loyalty. But please let him be right about Red Boy.

Then we take ourselves off to our beds. On the way up the stairs Garnet gives me a shy little pat on the shoulder. That just about undoes me, and I run down the hall and slam my door so I won't start blubbering right in front of him.

twenty-four

Days flash on by. The farm's not sold yet, but I have a sinking feeling I'm not going to get back there by Christmas. This gives me an awful twinge, but now is probably Michael's busiest season, what with keeping an eye on all the celebrations here on earth, let alone taking care of whatever goings on they get up to in heaven. Besides, I can't expect to reach the top of his to-do list until he gets to know me better. What I *should* do is be shining good as gold all season, and I bet I'll make number one as soon as the holidays are over.

I take the thirty-five dollars I got from selling the soldiers and go out to buy presents. I wonder about getting something for my dear ones at the farm, but the best present of all would be if I could just get back there. Better to save what money I can for Willow. I make a quick stop at the pet store for a spray of millet for Petey. Then I go to the candy store and get five Belgian chocolate cigars for Dave and a little box of chocolates for Dulcie. I'd get lemon drops for Moira because she likes yellow, but I've never seen her eat anything remotely sweet. I'm passing the window display at the Sally Ann store when I notice a shiny silver sleigh bell hanging from a red velvet bow. Moira would love that! She's already decking the house with spruce boughs and cedar. She could put it on the front door or over the fireplace, or maybe she could dangle it off Petey's cage.

I weave through the crush of people pushing both ways through the doors and slide over to the clerk who's working nearest the window. She's bagging purchases for the cashier. *Stuff, stuff, stuff,* she stuffs the bags, over and over. Her shoulders slump, and she shifts awkwardly from foot to foot, as if her shoes are pinching.

"That bell in the window . . ." I begin.

"Window displays come down on Fridays."

"It's for a Christmas present."

"Friday, I told you." She bends down and comes up with a cardboard carton. "How about I put everything in here?" she says to a very pregnant woman with a baby in her arms.

"If I give you my name, can you hold it for me?" I plead.

"Could someone help me out to the car?" the woman asks.

"We're short-staffed," the clerk says to her, and to me, "We don't take names." She grabs a handful of toys to dump them into the carton and knocks a box off the counter. Hundreds of tiny Lego pieces burst out and scatter across the floor.

"Oh, no!" the woman cries helplessly. The baby begins to wriggle and fuss. I scramble around among the comings and goings of feet until I manage to pick up most of the pieces. "Thanks," she says. "I can't tell you how grateful I am."

"No trouble." I heft the carton off the counter and follow her outside, curling my tongue and rolling my eyes until the baby laughs at me over her shoulder. I'm an expert at comforting babies because of all my practice with Meg.

Then I thread back into the store and wander around, picking stuff up, putting it down. But I can't find anything for Moira that's better than lemon drops, which she probably wouldn't even like. I need cheering up, so I head for the book section for a time-out. Here's a neat picture book, small and almost square. I like square things. Same up, same across, everything even. Stable, reliable, good old square. The pictures are filled with squares, too, making grids on the background in pretty pastel colors. A man with a piano floats across the pages. Thelonius Monk. What a weird name. Here's my present for Garnet! And on the way to the checkout I find a hummingbird feeder, its plastic cover only a little bit faded, which is the perfect gift for Willow.

The bagging clerk is working the cash register now. When she sees me coming, she reaches under the counter and pulls out the bell and velvet bow. "It's Christmas, after all," she says.

I offer her one of Dave's cigars. She shakes her head. "I couldn't take it."

"It's Christmas, after all," I say. Dave will never miss it.

"So it is." She slips the cigar into the pocket of her smock and bumps her eyebrows up and down. I take my bag of purchases and count my change. I have twenty-two dollars plus a few coins.

In the glass case below the cash register, rows and rows of earrings sparkle invitingly. Willow might like a pair of those as well as the hummingbird feeder. Now that she's safe at the shelter she can care about looking pretty. I'm planning on visiting her as soon as school's out. Or maybe she'd like some perfume. Or maybe money's still the best. I don't know how to make up my mind, so I leave the earrings and head for home.

When I get to the park where the tent city is, I cross to the other side of the street and keep a wary watch out for Dag because I've got all this money. I don't see any sign of him, and I'm just starting to breathe freely, when my heart falls dead in my chest. Down among the tents I see the unmistakable flash of a plaid blanket. "Willow!" I dash across the street and catch up to her.

One whole side of her face is stained with the yellowish clouds of old bruises. "What do you want?" she asks warily.

"They told me you'd gone to a shelter." The minute I say it I wish I hadn't.

"I'm back. So what? What business is it of yours, or theirs, or anybody's?"

I retreat a step. "None. None at all."

"I can do what I want."

"Sure. Yes. Absolutely." I keep my face as mild as I can so as not to set her off. "I'm glad to see you."

Her face softens. "Thanks."

"You were right, you know. I started out wanting to get an angel, but now I really do care about you. Even if I don't get one."

"What are you talking about?"

"Being friends."

"You're a funny kid, you know that?"

"What about Dag?" I can't stop myself asking. "Aren't you afraid?"

She sighs. "Nobody's perfect. He never meant to hurt me. He was sick the day that . . ." Her fingers trace the edge of the swollen place under her eye. "And anyway, he needs me. I missed that at the shelter. You're nobody unless somebody needs you."

Dag comes up. He puts an owning arm around Willow's shoulder and spears me with a suspicious look. It makes me so nervous I forget completely that I was meaning to give Willow the choice of getting a present, and offer him my leftover money. He counts it in a flash.

I start apologizing. "I wish it was more. The lady in the secondhand store said she'd give me fifty, but in the end she only gave me thirty-five, and I had to spend some on Christmas presents."

"Mrs. Cristo!" He says it like a swear word. "Next time you go selling things, I'll go with you. I'll keep her straight."

I shake my head. "I didn't like it there."

"You'll get used to it. I'll—" Someone calls his name from the far side of the field. He waves an acknowledgment and swaggers off to join his friend.

A sigh of relief floods out of me. Then I remember the earrings. "I got you a present already," I tell Willow. "It's here." I hold up the shopping bag and waggle it invitingly. "I think you're really going to like it. Do you want to peek?"

"It's not important." She's watching Dag with hungry eyes.

"Would you like some earrings, too? I saw some really nice ones at the Sally Ann, and I'll get one more allowance before Christmas." She touches her earlobes. I can see little prick holes where they used to be pierced. "There were some red ones that looked almost like real rubies. Ruby was my mom's name. Or you could come and choose with me. Wouldn't that be fun?"

She drags her gaze from the place where Dag disappeared. "You don't understand, Gemma. You don't understand anything at all."

I back away from the quicksand sadness in her face and run home, the stupid hummingbird feeder banging against my leg with every step I take.

twenty-five

When I get back to the house, I find Dave setting up an enormous Christmas tree in the corner of the living room. Garnet is helping balance it. Moira is on her hands and knees sweeping up stray needles. The whole house sings with a sweet forest smell. I'll bet it smells that way at the farm now, too. I wish with all my heart that I were home.

"Come help us," Moira calls. I feel like having a tantrum of loneliness. I feel like knocking their tree over and jumping on it. I feel like stomping on the dumb hummingbird feeder. I feel like screaming my head off. But what I have to remember is I've got to be good as gold, even when it's hardest, so Michael will get me out of here. One thousand one, one thousand two. . . .

I hide my presents in my room, and when I come downstairs, I'm assigned to string popcorn garlands for the tree. Once I get into it, I start to have fun. This was my job on the farm, and I'm an expert at it, if I do say so myself. I ask for cranberries, and impress everyone with my intricate patterns of red and white. Petey tweets cheerily. We have chicken wings for dinner, and we eat with our fingers, not minding the mess. It's the most carefree the house has been since I got here.

After dinner Dave lugs the huge cartons of decorations down from the attic. Then he and Garnet put on the tree lights, and we loop the branches with my cranberry and popcorn necklaces. Moira unwraps the boxes of decorations, all of which of course are familiar to me, and instructs us where to put them. Last comes the tinsel, which we have to put on carefully, string by string, no flinging allowed.

When it's all done, I get to turn the room lights off, and Garnet crawls behind the couch and sticks in the plug. The tree glows like a giant candle flame, and warm amber light pours everywhere. The tinsel turns and twinkles. Moira brings in mugs of spicy apple juice, and we all gather around the fire to eat the leftover popcorn and admire our creation.

Dulcie comes over to join us. "Doesn't it look lovely?" she says. "I don't have a tree myself this year. I'm going to my sister's in Alberta. Let her fuss with the tree."

Then Garnet says, "Tell us now, Dad," and everyone gets comfortable in a way that lets me know a story is coming. I settle myself, too.

Dave leans back in his chair. His face goes soft, and a faraway look fills his eyes.

"Every Christmas when I was a little boy, my dad would tell us this story on the night we decorated our tree. And when *he* was a little boy, *his* dad told it when they decorated *their* tree. And when *he* was a little boy, *his* dad—that's your great-great-grandfather—told it when they decorated *their* tree."

"It's a tradition, right?" Garnet says.

"A family tradition. Four generations old. And when you're a dad, you can tell it to your children, and they can tell it to theirs."

"That's five and six, right? Generations, I mean."

"So it is. You, too, Gemma."

"What's it got to do with me?"

Dave shakes his head and gives a little laugh. "I wish I could get this through to you. Ruby was my sister." He speaks slowly and deliberately, as if he were willing the words into my brain. "She was part of this family, just like *you* are part of this family. She heard this story many times. Now it belongs to you, too."

There's a pause in the room while everyone waits to see how I'm going to react. Dave still doesn't see that my family is on the farm, no matter what time my mom spent being his so-called sister. But she did hear this story, and if I hear it now, it will be like listening with double ears, hers and mine. I'll understand something about her. I nod my head. "Okay."

"Tell it now," Garnet says.

Dave cups his hands and examines the pictures there, then looks up and begins. "It happened during

World War One. My great-granddad fought in that war. He didn't see this story happen, but he knew a man who had a friend who did.

"It was the beginning of the war on what was called the Western Front. The Germans had invaded Belgium. The British Expeditionary Force—that's our side—was called to help drive them back. Some 70,000 British riflemen, the best in Europe, went out to face 240,000 German troops. They never considered how the odds were stacked against them, because everyone said the Germans were pushovers and the war would be finished in a matter of weeks. As it turned out, the war lasted years and many millions of people died. But that's another story.

"At first it was just the way they expected it would be—they were winning, and the Germans were on the run. But the French armies guarding the British left flank caved in, and the tide turned disastrously. The British were outnumbered by more than three to one, remember. Two small groups of them got separated from their comrades. They dug themselves shallow rifle pits and crawled in for the night.

"The next morning—August 23, 1914—the Germans attacked, swarms of them, pouring down from the hill. The Brits were forced back and back until, in the end, they were trapped against a river. There was no escape. They prepared to die fighting.

"All of a sudden, figures dressed in white robes, riding spotless white horses, appeared over the crest of the hill. The power of their glory blazed out around them, and their leader had shining gold hair. They carried no weapons, and they wore no armor, and as they galloped down the hill, their horses' hooves made no sound. The Germans turned their guns on them, and fired and fired, but the bullets passed right through them with no effect at all, and the riders just kept coming. The Germans were terrified. They panicked and fled. The astonished British watched them go, and when they turned back to thank the white riders, they'd all disappeared.

"The only explanation anyone could think of was that they must have been angels. It came to be known as the Miracle of the White Cavalry at Mons."

Mons? My stomach twists so sharply that a gasp flies out of my mouth.

Dave beams down on me. "It's an amazing story, isn't it?"

"Let's set up the soldiers now," Garnet says.

My body's turning to fire and ice with the dread of what's coming.

Moira jumps up and clears a place on the mantel. "Where's the box?"

"I thought you had it."

"I haven't seen it. Have you, Garnet?" Of course he hasn't, either.

They go through all the cartons, peering inside them, turning them upside down, shaking them. They open every box, pulling out all the loose tissue paper.

"I'm sure I packed it in one of these cartons," Moira says. "I always do. It must still be in the attic."

We all troop upstairs. "We're looking for a wooden box about this size." Dave makes the shape I know so well with his hands. "'Angel of Mons' is written on the top in gold."

I thought it was "Monster." I'm such an idiot. I punch my leg, and when it doesn't hurt enough, I punch the place again. But no matter how hard I do it, I can't blunt the trapped, sick panic rising in my stomach.

"It's an antique set of lead soldiers that was made to commemorate the battle I just told you about," Dave says. "It even has a figure of one of the angels who saved them. It's beautiful. You'll see."

I cringe inside.

"It's priceless," Moira says. "Part of our family history."

"Wait until you see it," Dulcie tells me. "Every soldier is different. Only five hundred sets were made, and each one is marked with its own edition number. And they're so well crafted, you'd swear they were alive."

How do I get out of this?

They comb the attic for an hour, upending boxes, emptying bookshelves, hunting behind stacks of old clothes, scouring every tiny nook and cranny, all the while growing increasingly more frantic. My body is so thick with guilt I can hardly make it move, but I fake looking, too.

At last Dave throws up his hands. "I don't know

where else to look." There are tears in his eyes. "You haven't seen it, have you, Gemma?"

"How would she see it?" Moira snaps, and then bursts into sobs. "Oh, Dave, I'm sorry. I'm just so upset."

He puts his arms around her and turns to Garnet. "You didn't take it into your room to play with, did you?"

"No, Dad."

"You didn't take it to school to show people?"

"No, I never would, Dad." His voice is high and helpless, begging to be believed.

"Of course you wouldn't. Now it's my turn to apologize. There's no need to start accusing anyone. The box will show up, I'm sure. It has to. It didn't just run off all by itself. It's in the house somewhere."

"Okay, okay," I tell myself: First thing Monday I'll go to Mrs. Cristo and get the soldiers back. Then I'll pretend to find them somewhere we didn't already look, under the sofa or something, and everything will be all right.

twenty-six

Monday morning as soon as the lunch bell rings, I race across to the secondhand store.

"Buying, selling, or looking?" the tinny voice crows through the speakers.

"Buying," I say boldly.

Mrs. Cristo shuffles her bulk through the doorway. The beaded curtain rattles behind her. "So, what does little missy want to buy?"

"I want to buy the soldiers back."

"Ahh, little missy has money, does she?"

"Not exactly, but I can get it. I can have thirty-five dollars by"—I make a swift calculation, counting up allowances—"the week after New Year's."

"Thirty-five. . . . Thirty-five." She seems to be tasting the words and finding them rancid. Then she cocks her head and pins me with her eyes. "Those soldiers are worth a pretty penny more than thirty-five."

"What?"

"You heard me."

"How much more?"

"Let's say . . . five hundred. Maybe more than that. I have feelers out."

My heart plummets. *Five hundred dollars?*

"Who knows? It's a very rare set, even without the angel." My knees go all watery. The floor surges up. Old fingers lift me. A sour smell clouds over me. Words hiss in my ear. "Those little soldiers are very, very special. Little missy should be careful what she lets go of. Let it be a lesson to her. A valuable lesson. No charge for that." Her body shakes with silent laughter as she pushes me toward the door.

I hardly have the energy to drag myself back to school. What happened? All I did was want an angel, and look at the misery I'm in. That old wasp, Mrs. Cristo—she was enjoying herself making me suffer. She's no better than the people who tortured the saints. Herod cut off Saint John the Baptist's head and gave it to Salome on a platter. Diocletian warmed his hands while he burned Saint Lucy at a stake. The Romans boiled Saint John the Divine in a cauldron of oil, and roasted Saint Eustace and his family in the belly of a brass bull. All through it, those saints never doubted themselves. No matter what was done to them, they kept their faith.

I didn't mean any harm when I stole—well, not stole exactly, when I took—those soldiers. It was for a good cause. The Archangel Michael action figure was a sign I was doing the right thing. I have to remember that. I must be brave as a saint and persevere in spite of my persecutions.

I'll get those soldiers back. I just have to figure out how to get five hundred dollars.

Christmas Day comes at last, still under the shadow of the lost soldiers. I haven't been able to get anywhere with my money crisis. I gave all my allowances and all my scrounge money to Willow. I did a lot of soul searching about that. I want to return the soldiers, I really do, but why should Willow have to pay for my messing up? And anyway, it's not enough. What I need is a big bunch of money all at once. I tried to buy a lottery ticket, but you have to be eighteen.

Christmas morning Dave and Moira make us eat breakfast before we open our presents. This would have caused a riot at the farm, but Garnet doesn't even raise a squeak.

There are so many presents underneath the tree, the bottom branches have to bend up to fit them all in. Still, everyone's eyes drift to the empty place on the mantel where the soldiers ought to be.

"Let's not let it spoil our Christmas," Moira begs. "They'll show up. I know they will."

We all make an effort to be cheerful, which isn't all that hard for me once I start opening my gifts. I get a lot of amazing stuff—art supplies, CDs, a pink watch and a yellow watch, a ski jacket, a whole bunch of decorated socks, a package of ten different designs of shoelaces from Garnet, and a box of chocolates from Dulcie.

Then Moira tells me that she's arranged for me to start dance lessons. "The blue fairy, as you call her, told us you had considerable talent."

"Me?" Clumsy me? Talent? I can feel a tingle on my forehead where the blue fairy kissed me.

"I wasn't surprised. I've watched you move," Moira says. She smiles dreamily. "I was a dancer, too, you know, before I went to law school."

"What happened?"

"I tore a ligament that wouldn't heal for a long time, and I guess I just got practical."

"I'm glad you did," Dave says, "or we'd never have met."

"It's worked out all right," she says.

La-lee, la-lee, la-lee LAH-lee, la, la, la, la, la, la, la, la, lah, toodly-ah. Sugarplum music dances in my head and my slippered toes wiggle in time. Imagine, me, a dancer! It really is too bad I won't be around here long enough for lessons. Never mind, I'll dance for Pippi.

Then Dave hands me a present he chose especially himself. It's a pair of red shoes covered all over with sequins, exactly like Dorothy's in *The Wizard of Oz*. "I hope you'll see," he says, "that this is home after all."

Not likely. But I love the shoes!

Dave and Moira make a big fuss over my little gifts, which are pretty insignificant in comparison with theirs.

"You've shown a lot of insight," Dave says, unwrapping a cigar and bumping his eyebrows up and down the way the clerk did at the Sally Ann. Moira hangs the bow and bell on the mantel and makes a fuss of how pretty she thinks it looks.

Garnet gets, among all his other loot, a gorgeous, ghostly, long white eel for his fish tank. When he first opens the little book I bought him, he gives me a weird look and flops it away as though it's nothing. But when all the presents are opened, he goes back and starts looking through it. I keep my guard up because I'm kind of embarrassed to have given him a baby book like that, and I'm expecting him to say something nasty, but he acts really interested. "Hey," he says, "it's a tune," and he gets up and takes it to the piano and starts plinking away. It's the first time he's gone anywhere near the piano since the night of the concert. Moira and Dave exchange looks, and Moira pats my knee approvingly.

I take quick advantage. "Can I call the farm?" A shadow crosses her face. "To wish them Merry Christmas?"

She sighs. "All right."

I rush to the phone. Before I call, I slip my feet into my Dorothy shoes, close my eyes, and click my heels together. "There's no place like home. Not here, not here. There's no place like home."

Meg is gone. How could they take a little girl away from her family right before Christmas? Social Services, you are doomed. Angel vengeance will be mine.

Now only Jess is left. "I think they're going to let me stay," he says. A pang of envy flares through me. Right away he can tell. "If there's hope for me, there's hope for you, too."

See why I love him? "What about the farm?"

"There's a Bible camp wants to buy it, but they don't have the money yet."

"How's Pippi? Do you think she misses me?"

"I don't know. Probably. I got a new skateboard."

"Merry Christmas, Jess."

"You, too, Gem."

"Can I speak to the A.'s?"

"I'll get them."

I call on thee, Archangel Michael: Keep the farm safe. Get me back there before I die of homesickness.

The next morning I'm up in my room packing for our ski trip to Whistler when I hear Dave coming up the stairs. I look out to see if he's hunting for the soldiers again, but he's jangling through the clothes racks.

"Where's my Eagle Crest shell?" he yells.

Moira comes running. "It's on the rack with all the other ski things. Let me look." But she can't find it, either. I duck back into my room.

"Dammit!" Dave shouts. "What's going on in this house? Where's everything disappearing to?"

"You'll have to wear this one," I hear Moira say.

"The collar's all worn!" he yells.

"We'll buy you a new jacket when we get to the hotel."

"It'll cost a fortune up there!" His feet pound down the stairs. "What's this world coming to? Guys begging for change at the liquor store are better dressed than I am."

Moira comes into my room to check how I'm doing and finds me doubled up on the floor like a salted slug. She kneels beside me. "Are you all right?"

Will this torture never cease? No, it won't. Just as we're about to leave, Garnet bursts in the front door. He's been packed for days, of course, so he's been out with a friend all morning.

"Dad! Dad!" he yells. His face is brilliant with news. "I saw the soldiers!"

"Let's go, Garnet." Dave spins him around and waves us all out the door.

"No, but, Dad, you don't understand."

"I understand that if we don't get out of here, we'll get stuck in rush-hour traffic."

"But, Dad. In that secondhand store on the Drive . . ."

Suddenly, the air is too thick for me to breathe.

"Just be quiet a minute," Moira says. "Let your father calm down. He's having a bad day."

But Garnet can't keep still. He climbs into the van and leans over into the front seat. "Gary collects old key chains, so we went in there to look for some, and the lady was showing a lead soldier to a customer. It was one of ours—I *know* it was. She was showing him the edition number on the bottom."

"I doubt it, son. First of all, that place sells only junk. Second of all, how could she have got them?"

"Can we at least stop and check?"

"Not now, Garnet. Not now."

"Dad!"

"That's enough! I've had it! Not one more word." Dave pounds the steering wheel.

Garnet flops back and buckles his seat belt. "It *was*. I know it was," he whispers. All the way up the freeway he keeps looking over to me and whispering, "I saw it. It was there." Moira tries to get up a game of Spot the Volkswagen, but no one's in the mood.

I crumple myself as small as I can on the other side of the seat. Was any saint before me ever thrown into such a pit of torment?

twenty-seven

Whistler Ski Resort is like a Pleasure Island of the mountains, with happy people in brilliant clothing zizzing down the ski runs, laughing and hugging at the bottom, and sailing merrily up in the chair lift to do it all over again. No one here except me seems to have a care in the world. Moira gets me ski lessons, and I hurl myself down the beginners' slope so recklessly that my instructor reports to her that I have the heart of a true competitor. The fact is, I don't care if I break my neck. It would at least put me out of my worries.

We go to get Dave another jacket. The whole of Whistler Village is rampant with shoppers staggering around with huge parcels under their arms. Christmas is hardly over. What could they possibly still need?

At dinner in the big dining room we can barely hear each other for the jolly chatter that seethes around us. When we finish, Dave pulls out his wallet and leaves a twenty-dollar tip. Twenty dollars! I take a covert survey of the other tables and see he's not the only one lavishing the cash around. This place is a gold mine. Here's my chance for soldier money on a silver platter. When we reach the elevator, I tell Moira I've left a book in the dining room. She says they'll meet me in our suite upstairs.

Our plates have been cleared already, but dinner hour is winding down and there are plenty of tables still littered with uncleared dishes. All around me I see plates and cutlery teetering on a king's ransom of large bills. I meander over to one that has what looks like a fifty poking out from under a half eaten bun, and sneak my hand up to the edge of the tablecloth.

"'Scuse me." A busboy pushes past me, clunks his tray down, whisks the bill deftly into the pocket of his apron, and starts piling up the dirty dishes. I sidle over to another table, but when I look up to check, he's standing with his hands on his hips watching me like a vulture.

If I could get the dining room to myself for two minutes, I bet I could pick up a couple of hundred dollars, easy. A few opportunities like that, and I'd be able to buy the soldiers back before Garnet drags Dave to the secondhand store. What I need is a diversionary tactic. If Jess were here, he could fake an epileptic fit, and while everyone rushed over to help, I could slide around scooping up the loot. Or I could set a small fire in the lobby, or . . .

I head up to our suite. I'm not in the least discouraged by not getting any money this time, because a plan of attack is taking shape. I just need to come up with the specifics.

When I wake in the morning, I know exactly what to do. Sometimes my brain does that—solves a problem for me in the night. I used to think it was just me being brilliant, but now I suspect it's angels at work. This is the idea: Call in a bomb scare.

That very morning, fate falls into my hands. Dave takes a spill and pulls a muscle in his shoulder. After an early lunch Moira takes him down to the fitness room for a massage. With no one to drag us out to the slopes, Garnet heads off to the video arcade in the basement of the hotel. This leaves our entire suite empty. I'd planned to use a pay phone in the lobby, but the one in our suite is much safer from the point of view of not being overheard.

I'm wrapping the receiver in a pillowcase to disguise my voice when I just happen to glance through the door into Dave and Moira's room and see Dave's big, fat, bulging wallet sitting on the dresser. Lucky me! In one leap I'm across the room and holding the mother lode in my sweating hands. How much do I dare take before he notices something's missing? Then my eagle ears catch the sound of the bedroom door handle turning. I deftly drop the wallet back and jump away. I'm not quite out of the room when Moira comes in.

"Gemma! You startled me. I thought you were skiing."

"Er . . ."

"Do you want something?"

"Oh, no. I'm fine. Really."

"What are you doing in our room?"

"Nothing? Just wandering around? You know?" Out of the corner of my eye I can see the wallet teetering precariously on the edge of the dresser.

"Why aren't you out skiing?"

"I thought I'd wait for you."

She smiles. "That's very sweet, but I might be a little while. You should head out by yourself. You're doing so well. You want to take advantage of every moment." She's right about that. "In any event, you know how we feel about the privacy of our room." She follows me into the living room. "What's that pillowcase doing wrapped around the telephone?"

I whip it off and flop it around. "Dusting!"

"Gemma, I really think you'd be better off—"

Behind her, the wallet plunks to the floor. I slip into my room and shut the door behind me. I hear Moira fussing with something and then leaving.

As soon as the coast is clear, I creep out. Dave's wallet is gone. All the more important to put my plan into effect. I wad the pillowcase back on the receiver and punch zero for the front desk.

"There's a bomb scare in the dining room."

"What?"

"A bomb scare. I mean a bomb."

"I'm sorry, I can't hear you. Can you speak a little clearer?" I give up on the pillowcase.

"There's a bomb in the dining room." I speak the words slowly, making my voice as deep and threatening as possible. "Everyone needs to get out. Now. Because of the danger."

I hang up. I'm trembling all over from the excitement of my daring. I'm thinking I'll give them a couple of minutes to get the place cleared out before I go down there when I hear feet thundering down the hallway. The door bursts open, and two huge men in black suits with walkie-talkie receivers in their ears shoulder their way inside.

twenty-eight

Three days later, we head home. The moment we get in the car, Garnet starts begging Dave to stop at the secondhand store and check about the soldier.

"It's on the way home, Dad. Please?" He whines it over and over.

Finally, Dave agrees. I pray for traffic to hold us up until after store hours, an accident—anything. But my luck's run out. There's even a parking space right in front. They all pour out of the car.

"Come along, Gemma," Moira says.

It's just about the only thing she's said to me since the security men at the hotel burst in on my bomb scare. "Come along" here, "Come along" there. Did you know that a hotel front desk can tell automatically which room a phone call comes from?

In the uproar that followed my call, I tried to pass the whole thing off as a thoughtless prank. This made me look like a complete lunatic. But I could hardly confess my true motives. And all the while, my heart was breaking because I was sure I'd blown to smithereens my last chance of getting the soldiers back. I was right about that. Dave and Moira never let me out of their sight the whole rest of the vacation.

"Come *along*, Gemma."

I ease myself unwillingly out of the car. What if Mrs. Cristo lets on that she knows me? If she does, my goose is cooked—might as well throw me directly into the boiling oil.

"Buying, selling, or looking?" the voice rattles through the speakers.

"We'll see," Dave says, very businesslike. Mrs. Cristo waddles out. When she sees me, her eyes widen in surprise, but I guess she can tell from the look on my face that something isn't right, because right off her lids come down and secrete her eyes away.

"What can I do for you?" she asks Dave, all charming and polite.

"I hear you had lead soldiers for sale the other day."

"Oh, dear me, no." She laughs flirtatiously. "Lead is against the law now. Soldiers haven't been made of lead since the mid-1950s."

Dave cuts her short. "I'm well aware of that. My son tells me you might have some vintage pieces."

"Very occasionally we're lucky enough to have the real thing pass through our hands. But not for a long time now. We deal chiefly in reproductions. Would you like to see some? They're very good."

"I tell you I *saw* it, Dad," Garnet insists.

"Our soldiers are very hard to tell from the real thing," Mrs. Cristo says.

"My son is a very good judge of soldiers." Dave's voice is sharp with authority. I've never heard it like that.

Mrs. Cristo throws up her hands and rolls her eyes as if she's only just realized what they've been getting at. "I know what he's talking about now. You were in the store the other day, weren't you?" She bares her teeth at Garnet in a grotesque imitation of friendliness. "I did have a few pieces last week, but I'm afraid a collector from Seattle snapped them right up." She shakes her head in a show of sympathy.

"Is there any way of tracing him?"

"None at all, I'm afraid. He was just passing through. So many people do, you know."

"Can you describe the pieces to me?"

I hold my breath. She doesn't miss a beat. "They were from a set commemorating the British infantry in the Boer War. Really very nice."

"No angel on horseback?"

"Oh, dear me, no. No angels. Shall I take your name in case I run across such a thing?"

"No, thanks." Dave herds us out of the store and into the van.

I close my eyes and lean back in my seat. The soldiers are gone, sold. It's finished. There's no way to get them back. An anvil lifts off my heart, and my body goes limp with relief. There's nothing I can do. It's out of my hands. I'm free of the need to get all that money. I can start again, clean.

Next day I'm in the front hall checking the key dish for change—nothing there, which is kind of odd—when I hear an argument going on behind Dave's study door. I hover outside and hear Dave saying something I can't quite catch, about how he owes something or other to Ruby, and Moira interrupting, "Dave! What happened with Ruby is over and done," and then Garnet floats out of the living room looking like he wants to glom on to me for something, and I have to escape up the stairs. An uneasy feeling starts to gurgle into my bones.

Later that afternoon Dave calls me into his study. He looks very solemn sitting behind his desk. Moira is there, too, perched stiffly on a straight-backed chair. Something's not right, not right at all.

He gestures for me to sit down, and reluctantly I do. There's a long pause, then he folds his hands on the desk and begins. "Gemma, your aunt and I have been talking this over. We're very sorry to have to say this, but evidence has been piling up, and we can no longer deny what we've been seeing." He takes a breath. "This is very difficult." He grinds his throat like a truck that won't start, *ehehhh, ehehhh, ehehhh.* I beat my heel on the leg of my chair to keep my mind off the dread that's rising in my stomach.

"For heaven's sake, Gemma!" Moira says. "Sit still, can't you?"

I quiet my leg, and concentrate on defending my feelings against whatever's coming next.

I'll sing you one-o.

When Dave begins again, his voice has the same sharp edge of authority I heard when he talked to Mrs. Cristo. "We believe you've been stealing from us."

Oh. That explains the empty key dish. My bones are dissolving.

Green grow the rushes-o.

"Shortly after you came, we began to notice money missing from around the house. At first we thought we must be mistaken. What could you possibly want with it? Your allowance is generous. If you needed more, all you had to do was ask. We still don't understand why you might have taken it. But there was no ignoring that it was disappearing. Then I see my jacket on the back of some beggar. At Whistler my wallet is obviously tampered with. A priceless set of toy soldiers disappears and shows up in a local junk store."

I half rise to protest that they never showed up, but he silences me with a raised hand. "Don't think I haven't been a courtroom lawyer long enough to know when an old con artist like that Cristo woman is lying.

"What are we to conclude? The evidence is inescapable. What have you got to say for yourself? Please let us understand what's going on. Why would you repay our kindness in this way?"

Fire rushes into my cheeks. I'm Saint Joan, strapped to a post, flames roaring up around me.

Dave piles on more fuel. "Honesty and trust, Gemma, are the basis of any decent human relationship. Honesty and trust. We leave money around because we believe we should be able to trust the people we live with. I don't know how it's been for you before, but this is how you will live in our house."

Moira opens her mouth as if to speak, but he powers over her. "There's no question in my mind, none at all, that this is where you belong. Make no mistake, Gemma. You are part of this family, and you will behave as such." He starts to count ultimatums on his fingers. "We expect an explanation from you *and* an apology *and* a promise that you will not betray our trust again."

Saint Margaret Ward was hanged, drawn, and quartered. Saint Julia of Corsica's hair was pulled out at the roots, and then she was crucified. Saint Blandina was meshed in a net and stomped to death by a wild bull. None of them bowed down to their tormentors. Dave and Moira can torture me with their words all they like. They can call Social Services. They can phone the police and charge me with theft. But they can't make me apologize. I'm sorry as sorry can be about the soldiers, but I had a good reason—which they are partly responsible for. I didn't ask to come here. I didn't want to come here. If not for them, I'd still be at the farm.

They'd better watch out. Many saints weren't recognized when they were alive. I might even be one, which wouldn't surprise me from all the torments I've been suffering. If I am, I might turn out to have powers. Saint Agatha could avert eruptions of Mount Etna. Saint Sebald could set icicles on fire. Dave and Moira might just end up being very sorry for treating me this way.

I face them down, my lips shut tight.

Dave heaves another sigh. "Your Aunt Moira and I are leaving for a conference this evening. We won't be home until late tomorrow night. Dulcie will come over to look after you and Garnet. That'll give you a day to think about this. When we come back, we expect an apology. You owe us that, Gemma. At the very least."

I leave the room, my head held high. What do I care what they expect? I don't owe them anything. It's not my responsibility to be the ointment for their guilt or whatever about my mother. If they think I'm staying here, they need to think again. First thing tomorrow I'm going back to the farm. I'm ripe for an angel, what with all my suffering, and Michael will surely find me there.

Oh, gee. I'm halfway to my room when I realize I'll need bus fare. I make a quick search of the house. Not a cent lying loose anywhere. I take a deep breath and go back to the study to ask Dave for my allowance.

twenty-nine

Early-morning frost crunches under my feet as I lug my suitcases one at a time across the lawn. All I'm taking with me is what I brought, but that means books, and they're mortally heavy. I've left behind my new watches, my CDs, my Walkman, and all my new clothes except what I need to keep myself covered. Moira threw away all my farm clothes except Jess's skate shirt, so I'm wearing that and a jacket—not the new one from Christmas—and some not very fancy jeans. My feet are bare inside my high-tops. I even pulled the fancy shoelaces out of them. I don't want to be beholden to this house for *anything*.

I do have my mom's *Charlotte's Web*, which is really mine anyway, and the Archangel Michael figurine, tucked away safely in my backpack. It's no use to the Burdettes anymore, and I do love it so.

I told Dulcie I was going out to meet friends for the day. She made me show her what I had in the suitcases, and I explained that we were planning on trading books. "It's like a book club," I said. That seemed to reassure her.

She made me wait for the batch of muffins that were just coming out of the oven, so I've got a couple of those making grease spots on a paper bag in my backpack. That's all. My life with this family is over. I'm free. I'll get out to the farm and work my miracles from there. I should have done that in the first place.

I get bus change by buying a stick of licorice at the corner store with my allowance. It leaves a lot more money than I need to get to the farm. I decide to give it to Willow. Anyway, I want to say goodbye. I head down to the park.

The tarp shelter is gone. The tents are gone. The people are gone. Squares of flattened grass and tracks of mud are the only signs that Willow or Dag or any of the rest of them were ever here. What happened? Where are they now? I drag my suitcases up Commercial Drive looking for someone to ask.

A man wrapped in an old sleeping bag on the steps of the bank tells me, "They tore the tents down Christmas Day. Sons of . . . Christmas Day! Drove everyone off."

"Who?"

"Who do you think? The cops, of course."

"Where'd they go?"

"The cops?"

"The people. When they were driven away."

He shrugs. "Downtown East Side probably. That's where everyone ends up when there's no place else to go."

"Do you know Willow? She wears a red plaid blanket, and she likes birds."

"Maybe."

"If you see her, can you tell her Gemma says goodbye?"

He helps me lug my suitcases across the street to the bus stop. I give him Willow's money and one of the muffins. "It's flat because of the flax," I tell him. "But it's good for you."

It takes me hours to get to the farm. I have to transfer twice. At last I look out and see familiar fields rushing by the bus window. I can hardly wait to get there. They'll be so happy to see me. I think I might paint my bedroom pink. The bus driver agrees to drop me off right at the bottom of the driveway.

"That's my house." I point it out, just visible on the crest of the hill. He helps me down the steps with my suitcases.

The first thing I see when I get off the bus is the SOLD sticker slashed across the FOR SALE sign—obviously someone's ugly idea of a joke. I try to yank it off, but it's stuck fast, so I pick up a rock and start whaling on it. It's harder than you might think to make a dent in a sign, so I settle for smearing mud from the drainage ditch all over it. I've got it pretty much blacked out when a horn blasts behind me, and there's dear Mr. A. staring down at me from the cab of his old pickup.

"What do you think you're doing?" he yells.

I fling my arms out. "I've come home!"

"Gemma! I didn't recognize you. What did you do to your hair? You look like a boy. And what are you doing here?" He's not as happy to see me as I'd pictured.

"I tried that place. It's no good there." I try to heave one of my suitcases into the back of the truck, but even two-handed I can barely get it past my ankles. He gets out of the truck and lifts it from my hands as if it were light as a potato chip. Dear Mr. A., so lean and strong. He swings the second suitcase up beside the first, and I run around to the passenger side and hop in. He starts the engine and rams the gearshift into first.

Suddenly, I feel like I'd better talk fast because he's chewing his mustache, which means he's upset, and I get an awful flash that he's going to turn the truck right around and take me back to the Burdettes. "Those people aren't my family. You're my family," I tell him.

The truck lurches up the driveway.

I kneel on the seat, working to keep my balance in spite of the ruts in the road, and yell into his ear over the whining of the engine. "It's like this. I get yanked out of here against my will—and your will, too—and I get sent to a place of strangers who don't even like me, and all I'm doing is missing you and the farm, and you're missing me. Because we belong. We belong together."

Mr. A. pulls up in front of the house and turns to

face me. The whites of his eyes are scribbled with little red lines. I've left muddy hand prints all over his sleeve. He doesn't bother brushing them away. When he finally speaks, his voice comes out muffled. "There's nothing to come back to. The farm's been sold."

Oh. The sold sign wasn't a joke. I fight back a gnaw of doubt. "It's okay. I have an angel. An important one. He'll fix it, no problem."

A breath goes catch, catch, into his throat. "It's done. It's finished. The New Horizons Church of the Rainbow Apostles has bought the farm for their Bible camp. They take possession on Monday. We'll be out of here tomorrow."

I follow him into the house. The kitchen is empty. The living room, too. The walls are bare, the curtains are gone, the furniture, everything. Just faceless boxes staring blankly.

"Ellie must be out back," he says.

Hunched in the back yard, filling it utterly, is a monstrous, gleaming motor home. *KEEP THE FAITH, BABY* blares in swooping letters across the side. We climb the steps. It's like a whole house in here. I recognize the kitchen curtains and the cushions from the living room. Mrs. A. is in the bedroom, plumping the pillows on the bed. I fling myself into her arms.

"Now, now. There, there," she says, rocking me and comforting my head. I close my eyes and try not to dribble tears down the front of her dress.

The kettle whistles from the stove. She peels me off

and leads me into the kitchen. I slip into a narrow U-shaped bench that curves along the wall behind the table.

"It's lovely, isn't it?" She sets out tea things. "We're going to travel all over. We've never been anywhere, what with the farm and all. We're going to Mexico next week!" She laughs delightedly. "Imagine me, on a beach in the middle of winter." She pours me some milk, drops a lump of sugar in her cup, and stirs. "This whole thing has been dreadful, but I really do believe it's working out for the best. Allan needs to take it easy. He's worked so hard all his life. The change of climate will be a relief for his asthma."

Asthma? I never knew Mr. A. had asthma. "I'm going out to see Pippi."

"Gemma, please don't be silly. The livestock's gone."

"What?"

"Surely you'd know that."

"You didn't keep Pippi?"

"How could we?"

I run around the side of the motor home and across the yard. The chicken house is open and cold. The barn is empty. I stand in the dusk of it and bathe my hands in a bar of light pouring down through a crack in the wall. If I can count the motes in it before someone calls me, I'll wake up and all this will have been a dreadful dream. One, two . . .

"Gemma!"

I suck the sweet animal air into my lungs and hold it

for as long as I can. I want to make it part of my body, so no matter where I go people will see me and say, "This is a girl who belongs to a farm."

When I get back inside, Mr. A. is drinking tea at the table, and lo and behold, sitting right beside him, wolfing a sandwich is . . . Jess! I flop down and snug up close.

He gives me a wink and elbows himself some room. "What did you do to your hair? You look like a boy. Pretty cute, though." I feel a blush fire up my face and I have to look away from his eyes so I won't fall in. "I'm staying," he says. "Did you hear? No one wants me except the A.'s. I'm going to Mexico for the winter. I got a passport. I'm getting home-schooled."

"You'll miss the farm, though."

"This place? Not likely. There's great skating in Mexico City. I can't wait to get there. You want the other half?" He slides his plate over.

"Okay." I shrug off my jacket and reach for the sandwich.

He grabs my arm. "Hey! You've got my skate shirt. I was wondering where it went. Give it back." He thumps me on the head. It's only playing, but it hurts.

Mrs. A. comes in, carrying a jar of wooden spoons. "You have to tie everything down in a motor home. It's like a boat that way."

"How do I get a passport?" I ask. "Or do I have one already? And where will I put my books?" No one answers. Then I realize—there's no room for books in here! Silly me. "Actually, I don't need my books at all. I don't even really want them. Just *Charlotte's Web*. It's only this big." I show them with my hands. "I'll keep it under my mattress."

For a long, stiff time Mrs. A. looks at Mr. A., and he looks at her, and Jess looks at his plate. Nobody looks at me.

Then Mrs. A. sits down, thump, and reaches across the table to take my hands in hers. "They're like ice. Always were."

"Let me." Mr. A. lifts my hands to his mouth and warms them with his breath. I can feel the light bristle of his mustache on my palms.

"Keep me." I plead the words onto his bowed head.

"We can't, Gemma," Mrs. A. says. "You have a home. You have a family, a real one, who want you. Even if we had room—which we don't—we couldn't keep you. It's the law."

"Please?"

"It's no use, Gemma. We can't."

I'm blubbering now. Jess puts his arm around my shoulders. "You can keep the shirt," he says.

thirty

$\mathbf{M}$r. A. drives me back to the Burdettes' in the pickup. By the time we arrive, we're not speaking. I'm exhausted from begging, and he's holding back his temper from having to say no so many times. He carries my suitcases up the front steps and puts them down so gently they barely make a sound.

"So," he says.

"So," I answer, and scrape my foot around.

He reaches out and pushes the bell. Chimes ring from the back of the house, and footsteps hurry toward us. At the last minute he gives me a quick hard hug, and whispers, "Whatever gets you through the night." For a second his heart beats under my ear.

Then the door swings open, and Dulcie flutters out wanting to know what happened to my visit with my book-club friends.

"It got canceled," Mr. A. says, and leaves me there.

I wave until the truck turns the corner and I can't hear the engine anymore.

"Did you and your little friends have a falling out?" Dulcie asks.

"I guess so."

"Dear, dear, dear." She peers at me sympathetically. "Are you getting a cold? Your eyes are all swollen. Have you eaten?"

I tell her I'm going to my room to lie down.

Saint Frances of Rome was married to a rich man who was something high up in the government. When rebels overthrew the emperor, she and her family were turfed out of their house and all their riches were taken away. Then a plague came. First her husband died, and then two of her sons, one after the other. She had nothing left but the clothes on her back, and no one to turn to for help. She survived by begging on the streets. Then she got an angel, and ever after that she could see in the dark by the light of its radiance.

What's the difference between her and me? I've lost everything, too. Where was my Michael when I needed him? And now it's too late. Even an archangel probably can't turn back time and unsell a farm. What have I got to wish for now?

I know. . . . If I could just get Michael's attention for one minute, he could get me a farm of my own. If he did just that one thing for me, I could take over from there. I'd build a swimming pool for Mrs. A., and a skateboard park for Jess. Mr. A. could work in the fields or lounge around, whatever he wants. I'd bring Arlie and Meg back home, and I'd free Darren from his chains. I'd fetch

Pippi Longstocking and her chicken pals from wherever they've gone. Willow could come there, and any of her friends she likes, even Dag—if he promises to behave. I'd put a notice on the Internet that all the children nobody wants can come and live on my farm, and I'd never make them leave. And something else even more wonderful— maybe while he was at it, Michael could find my mom and she could come live on the farm, too. Wouldn't that be something? But it has to happen soon. The A.'s are leaving for Mexico on Monday.

Okay, so what can I do to make it happen? In spite of all my best efforts, the farm has slipped away. I'm not good enough, I'm not generous enough, I'm not saintly enough, I'm not suffering enough. What does that leave me? Courage? I can't!

I bundle into my blankets and let despair swamp me into sleep.

Red Boy stands at the top of the rise. The sky above him is ablaze with the fire of his fury. He holds the barn overhead in one scaly hand and the farmhouse in another. Mr. and Mrs. A. and Arlie and Jess and little Meg and my mom and Willow are running around like ants trying to avoid his stomping feet. Then he crashes the house and the barn together, and the animals spill out, neighing and mooing and clucking and crying. They're under his feet now, too, and he's stomping on them. His tail crashes down on Pippi Longstocking, and everyone is calling me for help, and I'm behind this glass wall and I can't get to them and I can't look away.

I wake knowing inescapably that this dream is a sign, and the sign has been sent to tell me what I must do. In spite of myself and the coward I truly am, if I want an angel, I'll have to prove courage. There's no way out of it. If I want to deserve an angel, if I want to save the people and the things I love, I have to brave the scariest thing in my life: Red Boy. And where I'll find him is at the Only Seafood Café with its little neon seahorse. The Downtown East Side.

When Saint Margaret of Antioch was in prison, Satan came to her in the form of a dragon and swallowed her whole. The cross she was wearing around her neck grew and grew until it split the dragon in half. Saint Matthew said a prayer over a dragon, and it fell into an endless sleep. Saint Michael and Saint George killed dragons with their swords. They all went bravely and blindly into danger, and those without weapons went armed only with their faith.

I have faith. I just have to keep my mind on it. This is my faith: Tonight I'm going to earn my angel. I kneel by the bed and will myself to believe. Please, please, get me through this night.

Dulcie calls from the foot of the stairs that dinner's ready. I yell back that I'm not hungry. Up she comes. "You're going to fade away to nothing if you don't eat. Your aunt left a nice casserole." I let her shepherd me downstairs. I swallow and swallow, but I can't get food past my throat. Dulcie mixes me an eggnog, and I manage to get half of it down.

When we're done, she asks Garnet and me to help her with a little project. "I've got it right here," she says, and rustles a hefty parcel out of its wrapping. "Wonderball!" blares the writing on the box. *Your Easy Route to Home Fitness. Free introductory video included.*

"My sister gave this to me for Christmas. She swears by hers. We didn't inflate it when I was out there because how would I get it on the plane? But there's no excuse now."

"We've got a bicycle pump," Garnet says, "and we had one of those needle things for blowing up soccer balls, back when I used to play."

"You played soccer?" I ask. Skinny little Garnet?

"Up till last year."

"He's very fast on his feet." Dulcie says. "Very agile."

"So how come you quit?"

"I broke my wrist in a game, and Mom won't let me anymore."

"You're okay now, aren't you?"

"So?"

"So how come she didn't let you go back?"

"She thinks it's too rough."

"How dumb is that?"

"He couldn't practice his piano for three months," Dulcie says.

"He's not practicing anymore anyway," I say. "He should raise a stink until she lets him play soccer again."

"I used to really like it." He sighs and digs around in the miscellaneous drawer beside the stove. "I can't find that attachment thing."

"Never mind," Dulcie says. "We can't exercise so soon after dinner anyway. Who wants to watch the video?"

Garnet slides away to noodle around on the piano, which he's been doing quite a bit since Christmas, whenever Dave and Moira aren't home. I sit on the arm of the couch and consider how I'm going to work my escape. I'll have to wait until after Dave and Moira get back and everyone's asleep. I hope the buses run that late. Uh-oh. Bus fare. I grub around my pockets and come up with a dime and a nickel. I leave Dulcie to her video and do a quick reconnoiter around the house. Not a piece of loose change anywhere. That leaves Garnet's room. As long as I can hear him playing, I'm safe.

But when I get there, the burble of the water in the aquarium and the dreamy flip and gliding of the fish lull my mind so that I can hardly imagine where to look. At last I think to feel under the mattress, because that's where I keep *my* treasures, but all I come up with are Garnet's bone drawings. Yuck. I check all his drawers, and in his closet under his shoes. Nothing, nothing, nothing. He's got to keep some money somewhere; he can't have put it all in the bank. But it could be any-where. Short of tearing his room apart, I don't know what to do. I'll have to wait and bully it out of him when he comes up to bed.

I go up to my room to while away the time with my angel action figure. "Tonight you'll see how brave I am," I tell it. My voice sounds so thin and quavery it gives me the shivers, so I distract myself by galloping horse and rider up and down my legs and making like they're gouging the eyes out of the Bible campers who bought the farm.

"Hey, Gemma!" Garnet flaps through the curtain. "I finished another tune! It's way better than my first one. Do you want to hear—? Oh! What's that?" He's staring wide-eyed at long-lost Saint Michael balanced on my knee. "Oh!" he says again. Then, as realization dawns, "You've got it!"

His insect face bursts into happiness. "Where are the soldiers? Where did you find them?" He laughs and scumbles his hair and hugs himself and claps his hands. Then he starts bouncing around all crazy like a little kid. "We looked and looked! I thought I saw them at that store, and then—" Then he sees me paralyzed with horror and guilt at the sight of his innocent joy. "What's wrong?"

What am I supposed to say? "Well, Garnet, actually you *did* see the soldiers at the store, and they were there because I stole them and sold them for money"? I jump up and shove the Michael figure at him. "Take it. I don't care."

He pushes it away. "What's going on? What's the matter?"

"Look, stupid, the soldiers are gone. You'll never get them back." It's hard to keep from crying because it's so terrible watching the happiness drain out of him.

"What?"

"I took them and I sold them, okay? They're gone!"

He backs away. "You took them? You sold them? You mean you *stole* them?"

"Yes, I did, and now I'm leaving and I need bus fare and you'd better give it to me or I'll . . ." I double up my fist—"I'll punch you good." Tears are dribbling down my cheeks and my nose is running and I'm furious because I can't stop them, and there's no good reason for them anyway because I'm leaving this place and I'm getting an angel and everything's going to be great from now on. I grab Garnet by the collar and march him down to his room.

All the way down the stairs he's saying, "I'll give you bus fare. I'll give you bus fare to jail. I'll give you bus fare to Mars. You stole the soldiers. Who wants you here?"

I shove him into his room before Dulcie hears us. He pulls a fat dictionary off a shelf and opens it. Inside, a small metal box nestles in a rectangular hole cut into the pages. I'd never have found it there.

"How much do you want?"

"Bus fare, I told you."

"Take it all. What difference does it make? Just get out of here. I hate you." He's crying now, too. He dumps a fist full of change into my hands.

I shove it into my pocket. "I need a head start," I tell him. "I'm going to wait till Dave and Moira get home, and when they've gone to sleep, I'm leaving. If you dare breathe a word to anyone before tomorrow morning, I'll"—I look around for a believable threat—"I'll break your aquarium. I will. I'll kill your fish, every one." We both turn and look at the ghost eel gracefully twining and untwining its long body in the peaceful water.

"You wouldn't."

Of course I wouldn't. I wipe the snot and tears off my face, and growl through my teeth, "Try me." I'm just about out the door when I think of something to leave him with besides all this mess I've caused. "Here's a bit of free advice: Stop being such a wimp. If you want to play soccer, fight for it."

When Dave and Moira get home and come up to say good night, I'm buried under my covers, fully clothed, the Saint Michael figurine stuffed in my pocket for good luck, my eyes squeezed shut.

"We'll talk in the morning," Dave says, in case I'm awake.

That's what he thinks.

The house falls silent. I wait as long as I can stand to, and then I creep downstairs. A thin bar of light shines out from under Garnet's door. I tiptoe stealthily past. The door swings open. Light blares everywhere.

"You're really going?" Garnet asks. He's standing between me and freedom.

"Turn off the light, you idiot," I shout in a whisper. "And shut up." The light clicks off.

"I've been thinking. . . ." At least he's whispering now.

"Garnet, I don't care. Leave me alone."

He shadows me along the hall. I raise my hand to clobber him. "I'll yell," he threatens.

What can I do? I let him follow me down the stairs and out the front door. Then I give him a shove, and run. He runs, too. He *is* fast.

I stop to face him midway down the block. "Go home!"

"Listen, I want you to know, I'm still really mad about the soldiers—"

"You followed me out here to tell me that? Don't you think I know? Don't you think I feel like enough of a bum already?" I turn to go, but he jumps in front of me.

"No—I mean, yes. I mean, even in spite of the soldiers—"

"Shut up about the soldiers!"

"—I don't want you to go."

"What?"

"Leave home, I mean."

"Are you nuts? What do you care?"

"Nobody else likes my music."

"I don't like your music. I hate your music."

"You *clapped* for me at my concert."

"That was . . ."

"And you sang my tune."

"I didn't . . ."

"And you showed me jazz."

"Jazz?"

"And you gave me an A-plus on my bone drawings."

I try to duck around him, but he grabs my sleeve and holds me. "And you stand up to Mom, and, and . . ."

I can't get him off. "What!"

"You're the only thing in the house that isn't tame."

"*Aaaaaaaaargh!*" I scream it in his face and he lets go, but he sticks tight on my heels as I race away.

A woman is waiting at the bus stop. When the bus arrives, I stay as close to her as I dare so the driver will think she and I are together.

Garnet hangs on like a burr, and when I find a seat he scrunches in close beside me. "Where are we going?" he asks. I try to tune him out because I'm not exactly sure myself and I need to keep a close eye on the city as it lurches by outside the window.

Nothing looks familiar. Luckily the driver is calling out the stops. "Commercial and Hastings," he sings. His voice rings through the almost empty bus. "Hastings and Clark."

"Let's go home."

"Shut up, Garnet."

"Hastings and Campbell . . . Hastings and Princess." I listen hard for some kind of clue. "Hastings and Main."

Hastings and Main is near where Willow's friend said the women's shelter was. I'm up like an arrow and out the back door. Garnet is right on my tail.

The bus grumbles away, and we find ourselves standing by a wall of storefronts, shuttered and caged. What now? Opposite the bus stop is a big stone building with a crowd of people milling in the shadows around its wide, sweeping steps. Half a block away, a door opens and shuts on a snatch of country music, "I'm howlin' lonely for your luh-huh-huv . . ." Then there's nothing but the grating breath of the darkened city.

Garnet plucks at my sleeve. "Where are we?"

I remember what the man outside the bank said yesterday: "Where everyone ends up when there's no place else to go."

Then I see it, a few blocks down on the other side of Hastings, the pink and green glow of the Only Seafood seahorse floating above the street. That's where I'll find Red Boy.

I cross over, Garnet glommed to my side.

He points out the sign above the stone building. Carnegie Center. Shadowy figures dart and weave around us, shadows among the shadows, as though obeying the call of some eerie dance. Garnet stares, horrified.

I give him a good shake. "Go home, Garnet."

He pulls his cell phone out of his jacket. "I'm calling Mom and Dad."

I snatch the phone out of his hands and dash it to the sidewalk with all my might. It shatters into skittering pieces, and I stomp on them just to make sure. "Now listen! There's something I have to do, and I have to do it alone. Go home!"

"How do I do that?"

"Take the bus."

"Which one?"

"How do I know? Stop any bus and ask the driver. Use your own head for once."

"I'll wait for you."

"I'm telling you, go home." I start off down the block.

"I'll wait right here," he calls.

"Don't bother!" I shout it over my shoulder. The last I see of him, he's standing on the Center steps, a tiny figure marooned in the shadowy dark.

thirty-one

I run past yawning black alleys and boarded-up shop fronts and graffiti-spattered walls. Someone calls me from behind a Dumpster. It sounds like "You okay, kid?" but I don't stop to find out. A police car approaches along the wide, empty river of the street. I duck into a doorway, and when it passes, I go on. Across the street a crowd spills out of a bar. Someone shouts. A fight breaks out. The police car, lights flashing, whoops a U-turn, and everybody runs. I deke and dive from doorway to doorway until I'm out of range.

At last a puddle at my feet blinks pink, green, pink, green. I stop and look up. The Only Seafood seahorse fills the sky above me.

A tingle in my knees urges me to run on, run anywhere. When I don't, my stomach starts to heave, and I go over to the gutter and vomit up the eggnog I had for dinner. Red Boy is very near, my body knows it. But where? Oh, saints and angels, what do I do now?

The restaurant is shut up tight for the night and the surrounding stores stare out with blind, barred, boarded-up eyes. Then I notice an alcove tucked in beside the restaurant. At the back there's a door with ROOMS written across it in shaky letters.

I'm thinking I'll never have the nerve to go in when I hear a cry from across the street. I look over my shoulder and see a woman teetering toward me in sloppy high-heeled boots. "Arlene? Is that you?" She reaches out her skinny arms. I dive into the alcove, haul the door open, and escape inside. Stairs rise steeply into the dark. I take a deep breath and climb.

At the top I find myself in a long hallway half lit by a single, bare light bulb. At the far end, a sheen of pink and green glazes a grimy window. I walk toward it, past door after closed door. Behind one of them I hear angry voices. I pass on by. Another has a sign on it that says BATHROOM, with filthy pictures smeared across it. Glass shatters behind another. I pass them, too, and the room where somebody moans. I stand at the window, looking out. The neon seahorse floats just beyond, close enough to touch, if it weren't for the glass between us. There's a door to my right and a door to my left. The rooms behind those doors must look out on the seahorse, too. Maybe one of them was home to my mom and me.

I run my hand along the dusty windowsill. The paint is rough and peeling in places. I break off a bit and see, underneath the green top layer, a layer of salmon pink, and then a kind of gray, and then baby blue, and there's a feeling in my fingers of having peeled this paint before, and in my stomach of having seen these colors in this order before, and then the past rises up and sweeps me away.

I'm tucked up on my mom's lap. She bends her head, and her long hair sweeps around us, like a dark, safe tent. She's rocking me gently and singing:

> "I'll sing you one-o,
>   Green grow the rushes-o,
>   Oh, what is your one-o?
>   One is one and all alone
>   And ever more shall be so."

The air of her perfume is sweet as the breath of flowers. Her kiss is like the touch of stars on my eyelids. "Go to sleep," she says. "I'll be back soon."

"Don't go."

She untwines my fingers from her hair.

"But Red Boy . . ."

"Go to sleep, my baby, my jewel." She rocks me and rocks me.

When I wake, it's still night. Outside the window, a dragon writhes and flashes. I can hear him roaring, "Red Boy, Red Boy." The flames from his open jaws spill red, green, red, green, onto the mattress where I lie. "Mom?" She isn't here. "Mom?" She doesn't come. I rattle the door handle. "Mom! Mom!" I can't reach the light switch. The only light in the room comes from the monster's great mouth. I cower in the shadows as far from the window as I can get. I sleep and wake and sleep again. Day comes, but not my mom. I have to pee. The door is locked, and the toilet is out in the hall. I shout for my mom until my throat is sore. Night comes again with Red Boy roaring. I think I see a crack in the window. How long will it hold? He's breaking through. Another day. I'm soaked and dirty and hungry. Another night. I beat on the door, screaming. Then with a crash it bursts open, and a policeman sweeps me into his arms. His metal jacket buttons press cold on my bare stomach.

I never saw Ruby again.

Now at the window, tears boil up and spill. I'm afraid my chest will split apart with the pain exploding there. Then it's as if I'm floating on a little cloud, looking down, watching my body heave with sobs and the tears drip off my chin. I wonder if they'll ever stop. I don't care if they never do.

I watch myself cry, and cry, and cry, and finally the pain fades off and I hiccup to a stop. I'm all washed empty. Outside, the little seahorse beams nursery colors into the night.

Red Boy is gone.

In his place comes a rabbit hole of nothingness, a yawning chasm opening below me. My cloud tips me off, and I plunge down and down, into the hole, endlessly down. I press my forehead against the cold window and peer through the grime. The teetery-heeled woman is back across the street. I can still hear her faintly, calling for Arlene. *One is one and all alone and ever more shall be so.* So that's the answer to the question song. That's what my mom was telling me.

Now I know. I'm *One is one*. I'm all alone and I always will be. I'm not a saint. I'm not special. I'm just another kid abandoned by her mom. A piece of garbage to be tossed away and forgotten. Not worth a mom's going back for. Not worth the A.'s taking to Mexico. Not worth an angel's second thought. Not worth anything to anyone. A vision explodes in my head of a great fist picking up the world and smashing it against the cold, hard surface of the sky, shards of it flying up, skittering, like a cell phone hitting a sidewalk. . . .

I pelt down the stairs and out onto the street. A man with a bottle in his hand shouts, "Hey, girlie!" I dodge his reach and dash away through a red light. I run and run, block after block, nightmare far, until I reach the corner of Main Street. There's Garnet, standing on the steps, right where I left him. Below him, the shadowy dance of dark shadows continues.

"Garnet!" I shout.

"Gemma!"

Before I can reach him, a figure breaks away from the dance, catches my arm, and yanks me around. Dag.

"Well, well, miracle of miracles, if it isn't our little friend. What have you got for us today?"

I try to wrench free, but his fingers dig in, tight as

jaws. There's something wrong with his eyes. They're fever-bright, and staring wildly.

"Little rich girl." He grins and licks froth from the corners of his lips.

I hear Willow's voice. "Leave her alone. Let her go."

He begins to shake me, harder and harder. "What—have—you—got—" My head is snapping back and forth, and all I can see is the swipe of his evil face rushing past, up and down, up and down.

All of a sudden, he lets out a bellow and flings me away. I crumple to the pavement and look up to see him jerking and writhing above me, batting his arms around his head. Then I see why. Garnet's riding his back, clinging to his neck, jabbing him over and over with something in his hand.

Willow hauls me up and yanks Garnet off Dag. "Run!" she yells. We run. The three of us tear across Hastings and down along Main. Dag's heavy boots thump after us. Willow's blanket slips from her shoulders, and I hear Dag curse as he stumbles over it. We skid around a corner and up half a block to a gate in a long, barred enclosure.

Willow grabs the bars and starts to shake them. "Help!" she yells. "Help!" Lights flash on. Dag hurtles around the corner as someone comes running and swings the gate open just wide enough for us to squeak inside, gasping for breath. It's barely bolted behind us when Dag crashes heavily against it.

"Don't worry," says our rescuer, a small curly-haired

woman with a square, friendly face. "It won't break. I'll just call the police, shall I?"

Willow looks for a long moment at crazy Dag, kicking and screaming and hurling himself against the gate, then nods her consent. In seconds a siren howls up, and he's dragged off, cursing and shouting, into a whir of lights.

thirty-two

"That's enough excitement for one night," the curly-haired woman says. She shepherds us down some stairs and into a large living room. She hauls some comfy chairs up to the fireplace, throws another log on the fire, and settles us down.

"My name's Erin." She sticks out her hand. I shake it and so does Garnet, but Willow sits shivering, staring at the flames, plucking at the corner of her skirt.

"Where are we?" I ask.

"Powell Street Women's Shelter," Erin says. "You relax, and I'll get us all some nice hot chocolate."

My teeth chatter on the edge of my mug. Willow's having trouble, too. Garnet puts his arm around her and steadies her until her trembling calms. Erin passes around a bag of store-bought cookies. I lick the icing out of four of them before I realize what I'm doing. When I look up, she's watching me, but her eyes flick away, so I know she doesn't mind. I eat and eat until the sweet of it catches in my throat and I can't swallow any more. Then she brings me a glass of water and waits for me to sip it down.

When I'm done, she says, "Why doesn't someone explain how you came to be here?"

Willow stares at the fire.

Garnet points at me. "It's her story," he says.

He's right. This time it is.

I take a very deep breath and begin. I tell everything, all higgledy-piggledy, tumbling out any old how—about the farm and saints and the soldiers, about Willow and Pippi and Red Boy and my hopes for an angel. I tell about Dag and Jess's shirt and Mrs. Cristo. And then I tell about my mom, who tried to give me away when I was a baby and finally got rid of me when I was four. Tears bubble up all over again when I get to that part. "You were right," I tell Garnet. "She didn't love me, either."

"That's crap," Willow says. Her hands are still twisting in her skirt, but her back is straight and she holds her head high. "It sounds to me like she did love you. She sang to you, didn't she? She hugged you and kissed you. You said so yourself. You don't know she didn't mean to come back. Things happen to people around here. You don't know."

I wipe my eyes. Garnet sits beside me, quiet as a leaf.

"That's true," Erin says. "Nothing you've said means that your mother didn't love you. Many women here give up their children because they can't cope, not because they don't love them."

"I had a baby once," Willow says, and lowers her face to her hands.

Now the questions I've held back all my life clamor up to be answered. Did my mom love me or didn't she? Who was she? What happened to her? Why did she leave me? Where is she now?

"So, you two," Erin says kindly, "it's time we phoned someone to come and take you home."

Right away I'm on my feet. "No! No! No! I can't go."

"Why ever not?"

"I want to find out about my mom. Maybe she's wandering around the streets looking for me. Maybe she'll come here for help. Maybe she's been here already. Can't I stay? I could make myself useful. I could do the dishes, or answer the phone, or . . . or whatever you like. Anything."

Erin smiles and shakes her head. "You go home, and go to school, and get a good education. And when you're all grown up, you can come back here and really help—if you still want to."

"What about now? What if my mom needs me now?"

"I'll keep an eye out for her, I promise. But right now I'm sending you home."

What's *wrong* with this person? I told her my whole story, and she still doesn't understand. She's going to stuff me back into that house with Moira and Dave and all I'll do is run back here, and maybe they'll try to cage me at the Burdettes' or maybe they'll send me someplace else, but it won't matter, because I'll keep running back,

I will, and I'll end up chained to some bed somewhere because I won't stop running.

"It's not my home," I tell her. "They don't even really like me. They only got me because of guilt about my mom. I want my mom. They're not my family."

"What about me?" Garnet says. I look away, but his question holds me. He tells Erin the phone number, and she goes off to call.

thirty-three

Dave and Moira arrive in a flap of anxiety. They rush to Garnet and wrap him in their arms. I keep my distance.

"We didn't even know they were missing," Moira tells Erin over Garnet's head. "They were both in bed when we went to sleep."

"What happened?" Dave demands.

Erin gives me a look like I'd better explain, and Dave and Moira sit down to listen.

I stay on my feet. I don't want to tell them tender stuff. I don't want to go confessing and getting in trouble. "I don't know," I say. "I came down here looking for my mom, is all."

Erin takes me aside. "Believe me, Gemma, you'll be better off if you let them in."

"They won't understand."

"Have a little faith."

Where should I start? It's all a tumble. I look into the cup of my hands and see the image of an angel, making

211

bread. "I guess I could tell them the story of Saint Zita," I say. And so I begin.

Once I get started, the story seems to tell itself. I feel as though I'm walking through a long dark tunnel. The images step forward and speak and fall away into the darkness behind me. When I'm done, the listening faces around me are vivid, as though the space between us has been washed thin and clear like mountain air.

No one says anything for a long time. Moira sits still as a china doll. Dave looks at me wonderingly, as though he's never seen me before. Then he says to Erin, "Could you give us a few minutes alone?"

"Of course. Willow and I will be in my office."

They leave, and Dave honks his nose into his handkerchief and then he says to me, "I'd like to thank you for being so honest with us. It helps."

"What do you mean?"

"We've been so intent on rescuing you . . ."

"*Rescuing* me?" What's he talking about? "Rescuing me from what?"

He shakes his head. "We went out to that farm and saw all you raggedy children, and those hippies you were living with—"

"Hippies! They're my family!"

"Yes, well, we should have seen that. It's just that we've always thought of you as ours. You've been part of our family story for as long as Garnet has. We forgot we were strangers to you. We didn't stop to think how it would feel, us showing up out of the blue. And we didn't take into account"—he shrugs his shoulders around and blinks his doggie eyes—"what a complex and beautiful person you are. I'm truly sorry."

"I am, too, right?" Garnet says. "Complex and beautiful?"

"Yes, you are," Moira says.

"Dad?"

"Yes, Garnet, you're complex and beautiful, too. But we knew that already."

I mull the words. *Complex and beautiful.* No one ever said that to me before.

"Now, Gemma, is there anything you'd like to ask of us?" Dave says.

"*I* want to ask something," Garnet says. "Can I play soccer next year?"

Moira throws up her hands. "Garnet!"

"Kids mend. I'm not made of glass. You should have seen me wrestling that guy who was bullying Gemma. I launched myself off the top step, and I grabbed his neck, and I poked him and poked him with a sharp piece of my cell phone. Tell them, Gemma—tell them how I rescued you." Then his face goes fiery red, and the air goes out of him.

"Gemma?" Dave says.

"What I want to know is . . . Why did my mom leave me in that room? Why didn't she come back?" The questions erupt from my cracking heart. "Why did you take Garnet and not me?"

"I don't know what happened to Ruby, or why she

left you," Dave says gently. "I do know that she loved you both very, very much."

"Everyone says that. 'Your mother loved you. Blah blah blah.' But no one really knows."

"*I* know."

"What makes you so different?"

He scrubs his face with his hands and grinds his throat, *ehehhh, ehehhh, ehehhh.* "You remember I told you how Ruby came to us that first night carrying you two tiny babies? She came because she was afraid that Garnet was dying. He hadn't eaten in days. He was having trouble breathing. He was white and pale and barely able to move. We rushed him to the hospital and they diagnosed him with a virus and put him in a respirator. They said he'd likely be there the best part of a month. We all went home to get some rest, and in the morning Ruby was gone. She'd taken you with her, Gemma, and everything of value around the house that she could carry."

"Why'd she do that?" Garnet asks.

"We think she was having a problem with drugs."

"What kind of drugs?"

"I don't know, Garnet."

"Go on," I urge him. "Please." I'm scared of what I'm hearing and scared of what I'll hear, but not listening feels like *I'd* be abandoning *her.*

"Right. . . . A few weeks later she came back looking for more money and asking for Garnet." He stops and takes a breath. "No. That's not true. She wasn't looking for money. She wanted her baby. We gave her money. But we wouldn't let Garnet go."

"How could you treat her like that? You said you loved her."

"Yes, but you see, when a person's on drugs, they aren't themselves."

"You said you only *thought* she was on drugs."

"We knew."

"But it was still *her*." I'm arguing, but Mr. A. used to say the same thing: Drugs steal your soul.

"You wouldn't give me back?" Garnet's voice pipes in shrill with amazement. "Isn't that stealing, too?"

"Yes, it is. You're right. But what you have to understand is that we'd spent a month sitting by that respirator in the hospital, watching your little lungs try to work, watching you fight for your life, and falling in love with you. Now you were home, but you still needed careful tending. We couldn't imagine sending you off to the life you'd lead with Ruby. All we could think was how much better off you'd be with us."

"You didn't care about *me*, though." The words come out in spite of myself.

"Oh, yes, we did. Yes, we did. We would've taken you in a heartbeat, but Ruby never gave us the chance. We saw her often, but we never saw you after that first night. She wouldn't let us near you. You can understand why.

"We tried to help her straighten out her life, and we always gave her money, hoping some of it would reach you, but what was the good? Finally . . ." His voice trails off, and he grimaces his eyes shut and runs a hand through his poor, thin hair. "This is the part I'll never forgive myself for."

Moira puts her hand on his arm. "I'll finish. What Dave's having trouble saying is that, essentially, we drove Ruby away. We gave her a lump sum on the condition that she sign Garnet's adoption papers. I don't remember how much, but it was a lot of money to us in those days . . . and we told her not to come back."

I think of my poor mom banging on their door. Torn away from her own baby. "How could you dare do that?"

Her voice is strong and clear. "Dave's parents spent his whole childhood pouring themselves down the drain of trying to save Ruby. I wasn't going to see that happen to us."

Once we had this dog on the farm, a sort of terrier, not very big, a real yapper. They kept her for rats in the barn. I never took to her because she wasn't very cuddly. Then one year she had pups and the old hog came after them, and she went for him like a maniac. She bit the end off his tail. I liked that little dog after that.

Moira goes on. "Ruby came around a few more times, and then we didn't hear from her. We told ourselves she must have got on her feet and didn't need us anymore. Looking back now, maybe we could have done something better, but, truthfully, I don't know what it would have been."

216

Dave gives Moira a grateful smile and turns back to me. "When Social Services called us about you, it was like we were being given a second chance. We wanted so much to make up for everything."

"I'm glad you kept *me*," Garnet says, very small, and Dave wraps his arms around him. Moira joins them, and they cling together, safe in each other's embrace.

Suddenly, I want someone to hug me, too. I take a step forward. "I'm sorry about the soldiers. I really am. I know how important they were. I've still got the angel, though." I fumble in my pocket and bring it out. Its wings are a little bent. I straighten them as best I can. "You can have it back . . . if it makes any difference."

"It does, actually," Dave says, but he doesn't reach to take it.

Then I ask my last big question. "Do you think my mom's alive?"

He shakes his head. "I don't think so."

"I knew it!" Garnet cries, and he bursts into sobs and buries his head in Dave's armpit.

Dave strokes and strokes Garnet's hair, but his eyes are on me. "I'm sorry, Garnet, but she never would have left Gemma in that room if something dreadful hadn't happened to prevent her coming back."

An ancient knot in me unravels. Stray ends fly up and disappear. Tears rise and spill, but after the first rush of pain, I don't feel sad. More like . . . simple. Because now I know for sure and true. He's right about Ruby. She never would have left me. She loved me. She took me camping.

"What do you say," Uncle Dave says. "How about we go home, put that angel on the mantelpiece, and see where we get to from there?"

Then I'm in the tent of their arms, and I'm safe, too.

thirty-four

Willow hugs Garnet and me goodbye.

"I'll come visit," I tell her.

"Me, too," Garnet says.

Erin unlocks the gate, and we pass through.

The van is parked down by the waterfront. Garnet and I follow Uncle Dave and Aunt Moira across an overpass that arches us up toward the North Shore mountains across the inlet. The big question mark on the ski hill twinkles in the night air.

Garnet slips his hand into mine.

"I have stuff to confess, too," he says. I can feel the bones in his fingers, delicate as bird bones.

"You?"

"That I lied about when you rescued me from the bullies in the park. And . . . sometimes I sneak money." Ah, not so delicate after all. He gives my hand a squeeze. "You'll help me make a stink about playing soccer, right?"

A knowing flows between us. I can feel lines of loyalty drawing us close. I adjust my steps so we're walking in time.

Above us the heavy blur of overcast is heaping up and breaking apart around the beautiful, jeweled, motherly face of a full moon. Her bright beams rush like a river of silver across the backs of the opening clouds, transforming them into massive wings that embrace the sky.

"It looks like an angel, doesn't it?" Garnet whispers.

"Not looks," I say.

Is.